Luca's jaw moved as he swallowed. He was staring at her, his eyes unblinking. When he spoke his voice was low and loaded with emotion. 'It's been too long, El.'

Way too long—and the worst thing was that she hadn't even noticed until today. She reached out to hug him, as she'd used to whenever they'd celebrated an exam pass or saved a patient. But Luca's arms were suddenly tugging her in against his body, his head dipping so that his mouth found hers.

Ellie breathed deep, drawing him in as the heat and emotion swirling around them obscured everything in the world except them and this moment. Luca tasted of spices, of warm memories, and of hot male. Surrendering to the need clawing through her, she focused on kissing him back.

As suddenly as it had started the kiss ended. Luca abruptly dropped his arms and stumbled backwards. 'Ellie, I'm so sorry. I don't know what came over me.' And then he was gone, racing back the way they'd come.

Her heart pounded hard and fast while her hands shook and her skin tightened with need. *Luca.* What had they done? Whatever it was, she wasn't sorry. But she should be. Shouldn't she…?

Dear Reader,

Do best friends change into lovers gradually or with a resounding thump? I went with the thump theory! Luca and Ellie haven't seen each other for four years when they meet up by chance at an amputee clinic for children in Vientiane, Laos, and immediately both know their relationship has changed. Is it because of what's gone on in their personal lives over the past years? Or have they woken up to something that might always have been simmering behind their friendship?

Laos is a beautiful country, which I had the opportunity to visit a few years back, and Vientiane is a busy but compact city full of colour and noise that made me smile all the time. The market where Luca and Ellie go shopping also kept *me* busy, buying leather bags and earrings. Then I visited Luang Prabang, where the night market is fabulous and the earrings… Well, I have quite a collection. So I had to send Ellie and Luca there, which is a defining moment in their relationship. They visit the bear sanctuary and ride the elephants—and fall further in love.

I hope you enjoy their journey—the emotional one, that is.

Feel free to drop by and tell me your thoughts on sue.mackay56@yahoo.com or cruise by my site at suemackay.co.nz.

Cheers!

Sue

A DECEMBER
TO REMEMBER

BY
SUE MacKAY

First published in Great Britain 2015
By Mills & Boon, an imprint of HarperCollins*Publishers*
1 London Bridge Street, London, SE1 9GF

Large Print edition 2016

© 2015 Sue MacKay

ISBN: 978-0-263-26096-0

Our policy is to use papers that are natural, renewable and recyclable products and made from wood grown in sustainable forests. The logging and manufacturing processes conform to the legal environmental regulations of the country of origin.

Printed and bound in Great Britain
by CPI Antony Rowe, Chippenham, Wiltshire

With a background of working in medical laboratories, and a love of the romance genre, it is no surprise that **Sue MacKay** writes Mills & Boon Medical Romance stories. An avid reader all her life, she wrote her first story at age eight—about a prince, of course. She lives with her own hero in the beautiful Marlborough Sounds, at the top of New Zealand's South Island, where she indulges her passions for the outdoors, the sea and cycling.

Books by Sue MacKay

Mills & Boon Medical Romance

Doctors to Daddies
A Father for Her Baby
The Midwife's Son

From Duty to Daddy
The Gift of a Child
You, Me and a Family
Christmas with Dr Delicious
Every Boy's Dream Dad
The Dangers of Dating Your Boss
Surgeon in a Wedding Dress
Midwife...to Mum!
Reunited...in Paris!

Visit the Author Profile page
at millsandboon.co.uk for more titles.

This one's for Daphne Priest and
Diane Passau—two women I've known
most of my life and with whom I shared
many experiences as we grew up.

Thanks for the catch-up lunch
and may we share many more.

Hugs, Sue.

Praise for Sue MacKay

'A deeply emotional, heart-rending story
that will make you smile and make you cry.
I truly recommend it—and don't miss the
second book: the story about Max.'

—*Harlequin Junkie* on
The Gift of a Child

'What a great book. I loved it. I did not want
it to end. This is one book not to miss.'

—*Goodreads* on
The Gift of a Child

CHAPTER ONE

'PHA THAT LUANG,' the jumbo driver said over his shoulder, pointing to a stunning white temple behind high gates with two guards standing to attention outside. On elegantly crafted pillars gold gleamed in the bright sunlight. 'Stupa.'

'Wow, it's beautiful,' Ellie Thompson whispered. She even hadn't noticed they'd driven into the centre of Vientiane, her brain being half–shut down with sleep deprivation. *Wake up and smell the roses. You're in Laos*, she admonished herself. But she was shattered. *Too bad. New start to life, remember?* Probably no roses in Laos. Definitely no ex.

Right. Forget tiredness. Forget the humiliation of everyone from the CEO right down to the laundry junior at Wellington Hospital knowing her husband had left her for her sister. Forget the pain and anger. Start enjoying every day for what it could bring. There'd be no nasty surprises for the next four weeks while in Laos. She could relax.

Holding up her phone, Ellie leaned over the side to click away continuously until the temple was out of sight. Slumping back against the hard seat, she thought longingly of the air-conditioned taxis that had been waiting outside the border crossing at Nong Khai railway station. With the sweat trickling down between her shoulder blades adding to her unkempt appearance, this windowless mode of transport open to the air, dust and insects kind of said she'd had a brain fade when she'd chosen the jumbo over a taxi. But taxis were old hat, jumbos were not. Except right now a shower and bed were looking more and more tempting, and sightseeing a distant second.

Leaning forward, she asked the driver, 'How far?'

'Not long.' He shrugged.

Guess that could mean anything from five minutes to an hour. Shuffling her backside to try to get comfortable, she watched the spectacular sights they passed, nothing like New Zealand at all. Vientiane might be small and compact but there were people everywhere. Locals moved slowly with an air of having all day to accomplish whatever it was they had to do, while jostling tourists were snapping photos of everything from temples to bugs crawling on the pavement as if their lives depended on it.

After a twelve-hour flight from Wellington to Bangkok, followed by a thirteen-hour turned into sixteen-hour train trip to Laos, Ellie's exhaustion overshadowed the excitement only days ago she'd struggled to keep under control. Yep, she'd had a few days after she'd finished at the hospital for good when she'd begun to look forward to her trip instead of constantly looking over her shoulder to see who was talking about her. That excitement was still there; it just needed a kick in the backside to come out of hiding.

This was her first visit to Indochina and her driver was taking her to the amputee centre and hospital where she'd signed on until the second week of December. Ellie pinched herself. This was real. She'd finally taken the first step towards moving beyond the mess that had become her life and recharging the batteries so she could make some decisions about her future. 'Where to from here?' had been the question nagging her relentlessly for months. Laos was only a stopgap. But it was a start. Then there was the six-month stint to come in Auckland. It was the gap of nearly four weeks between jobs that worried her. Those weeks included Christmas and had her stomach twisting in knots. She was not going to her parents' place to play happy families when her sister would be there.

As the jumbo bumped down a road that had lost most of its seal the yawns were rolling out of her. Damn, but the air was thick with heat. Her make-up was barely sticking to her face and where her sunglasses touched her cheeks they slid up and down, no doubt making a right royal mess. So not the look she wanted to present to her new colleagues, but trying to fix the problem with more make-up would only exacerbate her untidy appearance. Nor did she carry an iron in her handbag to tidy up the rumpled look sported by her cotton trousers and sleeveless T-shirt. Today a fashion statement she was not. Hopefully everyone would see past that and accept her for her doctoring skills, if nothing else. That was all that was required of her anyway, besides being all she had to give these days.

Taking that train instead of flying from Bangkok hadn't been her wisest decision but back home it had sounded wonderful when the travel agent showed her the photos—highly enhanced pictures, she now realised. Face it, even riding all the way here on an elephant would've been tempting compared to living in the shadow of her ex and the woman he now lived with. Caitlin. Her sister. Her ex-sister. Her supposedly close and loving sister. Pain lanced her. The really awful thing was she still missed Caitlin, missed their closeness, the talks— Huh, the talks that obviously hadn't mentioned anything about both of them loving the same man. *Her* husband.

Sounding bitter, Ellie. Damn right she was bitter. Freddy had slept with Caitlin—while still married to *her*. She shook her head. The self-pity was back in New Zealand, as was the humiliation from having people knowing what happened. Putting up with everyone's apparent sympathy when most of those so-called concerned friends enjoyed keeping the hospital gossip mill rolling along had been gross.

But no more. Her contract was at an end, and nothing the CEO had said or offered had tempted her in the slightest to stay on. From now on she'd look the world in the eye, and make plans for Ellie Thompson. Taking back her maiden name had only been the first step. She liked her brand-new passport with its first stamps for a journey she was taking alone, in a place no one knew her or her history. It was a sign of things to come.

She patted her stomach. *Down, butterflies, down.*

Then they turned the corner and at the end of the street a muddy river flowed past and she leaned forward again.

'Is that the Mekong?' When the driver didn't answer she raised her voice and enunciated clearly, 'The river? The Mekong?'

He turned to nod and smile his toothless smile. 'Yes. Mekong.'

The mighty Mekong. She'd always wanted to see the famous river and now it was less than a kilometre away. 'Wow,' she repeated. She knew where she'd be going for her first walk in this delightful place. Another yawn stretched her mouth. That would have to be after she'd slept round the clock.

'I show you.' A sharp turn and they were heading straight for the river. Their stop was abrupt, with Ellie putting her hands out to prevent slamming against the seat in front of her.

'Out, out.' Her new friend smiled. 'See Mekong.'

He was so enthusiastic she couldn't find it in her to say she really wanted to get to her destination. Anyway, wasn't she supposed to be grabbing this adventure with both hands? Climbing down, she went to stand on the edge of the river beside the driver. It looked like running mud, nothing like the clear waters of New Zealand rivers. But it *was* the Mekong. 'It's real. I'm here right by the river my dad used to talk about.' Except he'd seen it in Vietnam. 'Hard to imagine all the countries this water flows through.'

The driver stared at her blankly. Her English obviously beyond his comprehension. Or too fast. She tried again, a lot slower this time, and was rewarded with a glower at the mention of Vietnam.

'Go now.'

Okay, lesson learned. Avoid mentioning the neighbours. After a few quick photos she climbed back into the jumbo, fingers crossed they were nearly at the clinic.

The next thing Ellie knew she was jerking forward and sliding to the edge of her seat.

'Here centre,' her driver told her. He must've braked hard.

She'd fallen asleep with all those amazing sights going by? Idiot. Looking around, she noted the rutted dirt road they'd stopped on. Beyond was a long, low building made of concrete blocks, painted drab grey. A few trees that she didn't recognise grew in the sparsely grassed front yard. Nothing like home—which was exactly what she wanted, needed.

Out of the jumbo she stretched her back, then rubbed her neck where a sharp ache had set in.

No doubt her head had been bobbing up and down like one of those toy dog things some people put in the back window of their cars. Great. Heat pounded at her while dust settled over her feet. What was a bit more grime? It'd wash off easily—as she hoped the past year would now she'd arrived in Laos, a place so far from her previous life it had to be good for her.

'Come.' The driver hoisted her bag and headed towards a wide door at the top of a concrete step, where a group of men and women sat looking as if they'd been there all day and would be there a lot longer. It had to be the main entrance.

She followed him, pausing to nod at the lethargic folk whose soft chatter had stopped as she approached. When she smiled and said, 'Hello,' they all smiled back, making her feel unbelievably good.

Inside it was not a lot cooler, and as she handed the man his fare and a huge tip she was greeted by a kind-looking woman who had to be about twenty years older than her. She came up and gripped Ellie in a tight hug. 'Sandra Winter? Welcome to the amputee centre.'

As Ellie tried to pull out of this lovely welcome that wasn't for her the woman continued, 'We've been looking forward to your arrival all week. The doctor you're replacing had to leave early. Oh, I'm Louise Warner, one of the permanent staff here. I'm the anaesthetist while my husband, Aaron, is a general surgeon. He's gone to the market. You'll meet him later, along with the rest of the staff.'

Ellie smiled, trying to keep her exhaustion at bay for just a little longer. 'I'm not Sandra Winter. I'm—'

'You're not?' Louise looked beyond her. 'That explains the jumbo.' Louise returned her gaze to Ellie, a huge query in her eyes. 'I'm sorry. It's just that we were expecting someone and I saw you and made a mistake.'

Ellie let her bag drop to the floor and held out her hand. 'I am Ellie Thompson, your replacement doctor. Did you not receive an email from headquarters explaining there'd been a change? Sandra has had a family crisis and couldn't come.'

Louise slowly took her proffered hand, but instead of shaking it wrapped her fingers around Ellie's. 'No email, no message at all. Nothing.'

Yeah, she was getting the picture. 'It was a spur-of-the-moment thing. I used to work with Sandra and when I heard how she couldn't come I put my hand up. My contract with Wellington Hospital literally ran out the same week. It was manic for a few days.' Hard to believe everything she'd got done to be ready in that time. Getting a passport and visas had had her running around town like a demented flea. She'd booked flights, bought appropriate clothes for the climate and job and had dinner with Renee and two friends. No wonder her head was spinning.

Louise still held her hand. 'Forgive me for not knowing and thinking you were someone else. I am very grateful you could come over at such short notice. It can't have been easy.'

No, but it had already begun to act like a balm to the wounds left by her husband and sister. 'Believe me, I'm the grateful one here.'

'We'll debate that later. I'd better text Noi. He

went to the airport to meet Sandra.' She gave Ellie another quick hug.

When was the last time she'd been hugged so much? She wouldn't count the tight grasp the head of A and E had given her at her farewell. A fish had more warmth, whereas this woman exuded the sort of kindness that would make anyone feel comfortable.

'I'm very glad to be here.' *Where's my bed? And the shower?* All of a sudden her eyes felt heavy and gritty, her head full of candy floss and her legs were struggling to hold her upright.

'The children are busting to meet you. And the staff.' Louise finished her text and set off in the direction of a door, leaving Ellie no choice but to follow.

Of course she wanted to meet the kids she'd be working with, but right this minute? 'How many children are here at the moment?'

'Fourteen. But that number fluctuates almost daily depending on new casualties. Then there are the families who can't leave their children here, or can't get to see them at all so that we go out to their villages for follow-up care. I'm only talking about the amputees. The hospital annex sees to a lot of other casualties, too.' Louise sighed. 'It's hard. For the patients and their families. And us. In here.'

They entered what appeared to be a classroom. Ellie must've looked surprised because Louise explained, 'We have teachers working with the children who stay on after their surgeries. Some are with us for months so we try to keep the education going during their stay.'

Chairs scraped on the wooden floor as kids stood up, some not easily, and the reason quickly became apparent. Three had lost a leg or a foot. Looking closer, Ellie noted other major injuries on all the children.

Her heart rolled. What was tiredness compared to everything these youngsters were coping with? She dug deep, found a big smile and tried to eyeball each and every kid in front of her. 'Hi, everyone. I am Ellie.' She stepped up to the first boy. 'What's your name?'

'Ng.' The lad put out his left hand, his right one not there.

Ellie wound her fingers around the small hand

and squeezed gently. 'Hello, Ng. How old are you?' Then she nearly slapped her forehead. These kids wouldn't understand English, would they?

'Six.'

Six and he'd lost an arm. *And* he understood her language. A well of tears threatened, which was so unprofessional. Do that and Louise would be putting her back on that train. Gulping hard, she turned to the next child. But seriously? She really had nothing to complain about.

The next half hour sped by with Ellie sitting and chatting with each child. Not all of them understood her words but they must've picked up on her empathy and her teasing because soon they all crowded around touching her, pointing at themselves and laughing a lot. Over the next few days she'd get to know them better as she changed dressings and helped with rehab, but this first meeting was unbelievable. She filed away each name and face so that she'd never have to ask them again. They deserved her utmost respect and she'd make sure they got it.

'Ellie? Ellie Baldwin, is that really you?' The

male voice coming from across the room was filled with surprise and pleasure.

She snapped her head up and stared into a familiar pair of grey eyes she hadn't seen in four years. Mind you, they'd been angry grey then, like deep, wild ocean grey. 'Luca?' Her heart pounded loud in her ears. 'Luca, I don't believe this.'

'It's me, El.' No one else dared call her that. Ever.

As she stepped forward Louise was prattling an explanation about why she was here, but Ellie cut her out and concentrated on her old friend and housemate. Concentrated hard to make sure she wasn't hallucinating. Checking this truly was Luca Chirsky, even when she knew it was the man she'd shared notes and rosters with at med school, and more than a few beers at the pub or in the house they'd lived in with Renee and another trainee doctor. Time hadn't altered his good looks. Though he did appear more muscular than she remembered, which only enhanced the package. Bet the ladies still plagued him. Some plagues were okay, he'd once joked.

Finally she said, 'I haven't seen you in forever.' Wow, this was a fantastic bonus to her trip. A surprise. She shivered. A *good* surprise, she told herself. 'Who'd have believed we'd meet up here of all places?'

Then she was being swung up in strong arms and spun in a circle. 'It's been a while, hasn't it?' Those eyes were twinkling at her as they used to before she'd gone off to marry Freddy. This was Luca. He had never hesitated with telling her what he thought of her fiancé, none of it good. The thrill of seeing him again dipped. If only there were some way of keeping her marriage bust-up from Luca.

Not a chance. 'Didn't you say your name was Thompson?' Louise asked from somewhere beside them. 'I'm not going deaf as well as forgetful, am I?'

Luca almost dropped Ellie to her feet. His finger lifted her chin so he could eyeball her. 'You've gone back to Thompson, eh?' Then he deliberately looked at her left hand, which was still gripping his arm, her ring finger bare of a wedding band, and then back to lock his gaze on hers. 'So you're single again.' He didn't need to say, 'I warned you.' It was there in the slow burn of his eyes, changing his pleasure at seeing her to caution.

Ice-like fingers of disappointment skittered across her arms. So much for being excited to see Luca. She'd had a momentary brain fade. *Having a few of them today.* After all this time without any contact between them he'd gone for the jugular straight up. Guess that put their friendship where it belonged—in the past. She didn't understand why. They'd been so close nothing should've affected their friendship. The last person on the planet she'd expected to find here was Luca, and he knew too much about her for these weeks to now be a quiet time. She could do without playing catch-up, or the shake of his head every time he said her surname. Luca would cloud her thinking and bring back memories of where she'd planned on being by now if she hadn't gone and got married. Plans she'd sat up late at night discussing endlessly with him until she'd started dating Freddy.

Even now Luca's head moved from side to side

as he said, 'Seems you're right, Louise. Ellie Thompson she is.'

Fatigue combined with annoyance and a sense of let-down to come out as anger. 'Are Mrs Chirsky and your child here? Or are they back in New Zealand awaiting your return?'

The expression on his face instantly became unreadable as he took a step back from her. 'Don't go there, Ellie,' he warned.

So he could give her a hard time and she should remain all sweetness and light. Too bad she'd forgotten how to do that since that fateful morning she'd found Freddy in bed with more than a pillow. 'Or what?' she snapped. Last time they'd talked he'd been gearing up for his wedding. More like girding up. There'd been a pregnancy involved that he definitely hadn't been happy about. Nor would he talk to her about it, or anything going on in his life then. He'd clammed up tighter than a rock oyster. Kind of said where their friendship had got to.

Louise tapped her arm. 'Come on, I'll show you to your room so you can unpack and take a shower.'

It was the worried look Louise kept flicking between her and Luca that dampened down Ellie's temper; nothing that Luca had said. 'I'm sorry. I must sound very ungrateful. I'd really like to see where I'm staying.' She didn't want Louise thinking her and Luca couldn't work together, because they could. It would just be a matter of remaining professional and ignoring the past. Easy as.

Luca picked up her bag before she could make a move. 'I'll take that.'

Louise scowled. 'Maybe you could catch up with Ellie later when she's had some sleep.'

To lighten the atmosphere that she'd created just by being here, Ellie forced a laugh. 'Trust me, there won't be any talking about anything past, present or future for the next twenty-four hours. I'm all but comatose on my feet. The sooner I can lie down, the better. I got no sleep at all on the train from Bangkok. The carriage was too noisy and stuffy.'

Luca draped an arm over her shoulders. 'That's what planes are for, El. They're comfortable and fast, and the cabin crew even feeds you.' Back to being less antagonistic, then. His use of El was a clue.

'Remind me of that later when I come up with some other hare-brained scheme for getting home.' She'd left booking flights as she had no idea what she might want to do next, where she might go to fill in the weeks between this job and the position she was taking up early in January. Following Louise, Luca's arm still on her shoulders and feeling heavy, yet strong and familiar, she sucked in on her confusion. Maybe she did need familiar right now. Maybe her old friend could help her by going back over that time when she'd made the monumental error of thinking she loved Freddy more than her future and wanted to spend the rest of her life with him. Now she wanted to reroute her life and, if she stopped being so defensive, talking to Luca might turn out to be the fix she needed. If he didn't rub her nose in what had happened, they should be able to get along just fine. Surely their past friendship counted for something?

Then heat prickled Ellie's skin. Damn, but she needed a shower. She probably smelled worse than roadkill that had been left in the sun for days. Except this heat felt different from what she'd been experiencing all morning.

She shrugged away from Luca's arm and straightened up the sags in her body. 'I'm looking forward to catching up.' She smiled at Luca. The heat intensified when he smiled back. Most unusual. Had to be excitement over seeing him again, despite the shaky start. 'But not today.'

Might as well go for friendly; after all they used to be very good at it. There'd been a time, when they were sharing that house, that there was little they didn't know about each other. At one point just before they'd finished their first year as junior doctors she'd wondered if they might've had a fling. They'd seemed attracted to each other in a way they'd never been before, and then she'd met Freddy and that had been that. Eventually she'd moved to Wellington and lost contact with Luca and the others she'd lived with for so long, until the beginning of the year when she'd caught up with Renee and now shared an apartment with her. Ellie had presumed Luca had married and become a father. Seemed she'd been wrong.

Thankfully today she could categorically state she felt no attraction for Luca at all. Not a drop. That heat had been something out of the blue. Hell, today she was struggling with the friendship thing after the way he'd looked at her with that 'I told you so' in his sharp eyes. It made her want to grind her teeth and kick him in the shin. It reminded her how he used to be so positive about diagnoses when they were junior doctors. That was 'the look' he'd become known for. Unfortunately he was more often right than wrong about everything.

Just like his prediction about her ex. Except not even Luca had got it as bad or humiliating as the demise of her marriage had turned out to be.

CHAPTER TWO

'KNOCK ME OVER,' Luca muttered as he stood back for Ellie and Louise to enter the small room that would be El's home for the next month. Ellie Thompson had popped up out of nowhere in full splendour, if a little bedraggled around the edges. All that thick, dark blonde hair still long and gleaming, while her eyes watched everything and everyone, though now there was a wariness he'd never seen before. 'Your smile's missing.' Did he really say that out loud?

Ellie lifted those eyes to him and he saw her weariness. 'It's probably back in the third carriage of the overnight train I was on.'

Somehow Luca didn't believe her exhaustion was all to do with her trip. It appeared ingrained in her bones and muscles as well as deep in those hazel eyes, even in her soul. So not the Ellie he used to know and had had a lot of fun with.

What had Baldwin done to her? Played around behind her back? That had always been on the cards. The guy had never been able to keep his pants zipped, even when he'd first started dating Ellie. It had broken Luca's heart when Ellie had told him the guy loved her and was over being the playboy since he'd asked her to marry him. The old 'leopard and its spots' story. But she hadn't wanted to hear what he could've told her. Then his own problems had exploded in his face and he'd been too caught up dealing with Gaylene's lies and conniving to notice Ellie's departure.

Placing her bag on the desk, he turned for the door. 'We'll catch up when you've had forty winks.'

'Make that a thousand and forty.'

'You okay, El? Like, really deep down okay?' he asked, worry latching on to him. They might've been out of touch but she used to be his closest friend. He'd never replaced her and would still do anything for her—if only she ever asked.

Her eyes were slits as that hazel shade glittered

at him. 'Never been better,' she growled. 'Now, can you leave me to settle in?'

'On my way. Or do you want me to show you where the showers are?'

'I'll do that.' Louise stepped between them. Putting a hand on his arm, she pushed lightly. 'Go check up on little Hoppy.' Then her phone rang and she stepped away. After listening for a few seconds she said, 'Hang on. Sorry, Ellie, I'll be a couple of minutes. Aaron left the shopping list in the kitchen.'

Ellie's shoulders slumped as she watched Louise bustle away. 'All I want is a shower and some sleep.'

Luca's heart rolled over for her so he reached out for her hand and gently tugged her close. 'Come on, grab your toiletries and that towel and I'll show you where to go.'

She did as he said, silently. What had that man done? Or was this truly just jet lag and a sleepless night on the train making her like this? 'El, while you're showering I'll make you a sandwich and grab a bottle of water. You must be starving.'

'You still call me El.' Now there was a glim-

mer of a smile touching her lips. 'I'm fraction-
ally shorter and nowhere near as beautiful as
the model you wanted to compare me with. I'm
fatter too.'

'The hell you are. You're thinner than I've ever
seen you.' And he didn't like it.

The smile fell away, and she shivered. 'I
needed to lose weight.'

'I'll have to start calling you stick insect.' He
grinned to show he was teasing, something he'd
never had to do before when they'd spent a lot
of time together. But he needed to know what
was going on. Something had happened to her.
He'd swear it.

'I've been called worse.' Distress blinked out
at him.

He opened his mouth without thinking about
what he'd say. 'Who by?' When she winced he
draped an arm over her shoulders to hold her
in against him as they walked along the path to
the ablutions block. 'What did that scumbag do
to you?' he asked next, struggling to hold onto
a rare anger.

Just like that, crabby Ellie returned. Her back

straightened as she yanked her shoulders free of his arm. The face she turned on his was red and tight, her eyes sparking like a live wire. A dangerous live wire. 'You haven't told me if your wife's living over here with you.'

She fought dirty, he'd give her that. Her being Ellie, that meant she was hiding something. Stepping farther away from her, he waved along the path. 'Third door down are the showers. I'll get one of the kids to put that sandwich and water in your room.' He spun away to stride towards the clinic, where he could bury himself in patients' problems and not worry about what might've happened to Ellie. Strange, but for a long time he hadn't thought about what Gaylene had tried to do to him all those years ago, certainly not since he'd arrived here. It wasn't as though Ellie and Gaylene went hand in hand, but the friendship he'd had with El had gone belly up at that time.

'Luca.' A soft hand touched his biceps. 'Luca, stop, please.'

He turned midstride to face Ellie, and instantly

his anger dissipated. It wasn't her fault that he'd been made a fool of way back then. 'I'm sorry.'

'Me, too.' Ellie huffed a long sigh. 'I got such a shock seeing you across the room, and I don't seem to have returned to normal since. I don't want to fight with you. We were never very good at that, and starting now doesn't make a lot of sense.'

'I guess four years is a long time, with many things having gone down for each of us. Let's go back to when we were happy being pals and downing beers as if it was going out of fashion on our days off.' He'd like that more than anything right about now. A cold beer—with his pal. They had a lot of catching up to do. And not just the bad stuff.

Ellie nodded slowly. 'That'd be great. A friend is what I really need more than anything.'

Don't ask. 'Done.' He followed through on his previous thought. 'Get some shut-eye and tonight we'll go to a bar in town for a reunion beer or two. Then you can catch up on some more sleep before you start to get to know your way around here. How does that sound?' He held his breath.

At last. A full-blown Ellie smile came his way, like warm hands around his heart. 'Perfect.' She started to move past him.

Luca suddenly felt the need to tell her. To get it out of the way, because it would hang between them like an unsolved puzzle if he avoided the issue, and he didn't want that. 'I never married her.'

She nearly lost her balance, and when she raised her face to him her eyes were wide. But she kept quiet, waiting for him to finish his story.

As if that could be told in thirty seconds, but he supposed he could give her the bones of it. 'She terminated the baby. Said she'd met someone else and didn't want to take my child into that relationship.' If it had been his child. She hadn't exactly been monogamous with him. He would've insisted on a DNA test being done but he'd been trying to trust her and accept what had happened.

He'd always been supercareful about using condoms during every liaison. But no child of his would ever grow up without his father at his side, and that edict had taken him straight into Gaylene's hands—until she'd found a richer man. Luca's hands fisted on his hips, as they always did when he thought about that selfish woman. The only good thing she had done was remind him exactly why he had no intention of ever, ever getting married or having children.

'You always said you weren't going to marry or have children. I was surprised when I heard about the circumstances of your wedding, but so many people get caught out by an unplanned pregnancy.' Ellie leaned against him. 'I should've phoned then.'

But by then he'd told her what he thought of her marrying Baldwin. He got it. She'd still been angry with him. 'We were both tied up with our careers and finishing exams, not to mention other things. There was a lot going on.' *I wouldn't have told you anyway. Like I've never told you about my father and my grandfather and how they let down those nearest and dearest big time. How my father took his would-be father-in-law's propensity for deserting his wife and children to a whole new level.* Some things were best kept in the family.

Ellie nodded. 'Our friendship was under a fair bit of strain, if I remember rightly.'

'You do.' But he wouldn't raise the subject that had come between them again. Not today anyhow. 'Go shower and head to bed. Your eyeballs are hanging halfway down your face. I'll warn everyone to be quiet around your room.'

'Nice. How come I didn't scare the kids, then? I must look very ugly.' Her smile slipped as a yawn gripped her.

'They're a lot tougher than you'd guess.' Luca felt his usual sadness for these beautiful and gentle people who dealt with so much, then he glanced at Ellie and brightened. 'But they're also very like kids anywhere in the world when you buy treats or play cricket with them.' Things he was always indulging in.

He felt his heart lurch as Ellie stepped through into the ablutions block and shut the door. El. His dearest friend. Damn, but he'd missed her, and he was only just realising how much. No one quite poked the borax at him the way she had whenever he'd got too serious about something she'd deemed to be ridiculous. She was usually spot on too. But now something was definitely not right. He'd never seen her so beaten, as though all the things she held dear and near were gone. Somehow, sometime, over the coming weeks he'd find out, and see if he couldn't help her to get her spark back.

Ellie woke to knocking on her door. *Where am I?* She looked around at the children's drawings covering the walls and it all came back in a hurry. Vientiane. The amputee centre. She stretched her toes to the end of the bed and raised her arms above her head. She'd slept like the dead and now felt good all over, ready to start her job in this country that was new to her.

Knock, knock.

'Who is it?'

'Chi. Luca said you have to get up. I've got you more water.'

Luca. So that hadn't been a dream. She'd be excited about catching up with him if she didn't know he'd want all the details about her failed marriage. He wasn't going to get them but he'd persist for days; she just knew it. Then again, he had told her why he wasn't married. What a witch that woman had turned out to be. Terminating their baby with no regard for its father. That was beyond her comprehension. But then she'd never faced a similar situation. Freddy had made certain she didn't get pregnant.

'Ellie?'

'Sorry, come in.' Ellie shuffled upright and leaned back against the wall as Chi entered.

'Luca said you're going out at seven o'clock.' The girl spoke precisely and slowly as if searching for the right words.

Damn, she'd forgotten Luca's suggestion of a beer in town. Taking the proffered bottle of water from Chi, she snapped the lid open and said, 'Thank you, Chi.'

The girl beamed as Ellie poured the cool liquid down her parched throat.

'What time is it?' she paused long enough to ask.

'Half past six. Are you still tired?'

'A little bit, but eight hours is more than

enough for now. I wouldn't have slept tonight if you hadn't woken me.' As Chi sat down on the chair in the corner Ellie asked, 'Where did you learn to speak such good English?' The girl looked so cute in her oversize shirt and too-small trousers.

'Here. The doctors and nurses teach me.' Pride filled her face, lightened her eyes.

'How long have you been in the centre?' To have learned to speak English to a level she could be understood without too much difficulty she must've been around the medical staff a long time.

'I was this high when I came with my brother.' Chi held her hand less than a metre above the floor. Ellie guessed she was now closer to one hundred and twenty centimetres. 'Long time ago. My brother was this high.' Half a metre off the floor.

'Is your brother still here, too?'

Chi blinked, the pride gone, replaced with stoic sadness. 'He died. The bomb cut off his leg and the blood ran out.'

Ellie shuddered. Reality sucked, and was very

confronting. Flying fragments of metal did a lot of damage, and were often lethal. It had been a spur-of-the-moment decision to come here. When she'd heard about Sandra's family crisis she'd thought about the weeks looming with nothing to keep her busy before she took up her next job and put her hand up. Helping people in these circumstances was so different from working in an emergency department back home, where life was easier and a lot of things like medical care taken for granted. Here people, many only young children, were still being injured, maimed or killed by bombs that had been left lying around or shallow buried decades ago.

'Louise and Aaron adopted me. My mother and father are gone, too.'

How much reality should a child have to deal with? Leaping out of bed, she scooped the girl into a hug. 'I'm so happy to know you, Chi.'

'Knew I couldn't trust a female to get my message across without stopping to yak the day away.' Luca stood in the doorway, his trademark grin including both her and Chi in that comment.

With sudden clarity Ellie understood how

much she'd missed that grin and the man behind it. Missed their conversations about everything from how to put a dislocated shoulder back into its socket to which brand of beer was the best. They'd argued, and laughed, and fought over whose turn it was to clean the house. They'd cheered each other on in exams while secretly hoping they did better than the other.

She ran to throw her arms around him. 'I'm glad I've found you again.'

'I'm glad, too, because tomorrow's your turn to do the washing.' He laughed against the top of her head.

His hands were spread across her back, his warmth seeping into her bones and thawing some of the chill that had taken up residence on the morning she came home from work to find Freddy and Caitlin in her marital bed, doing what only she should've been doing with her husband. She breathed deep, drawing in the scent that was Luca, her closest friend ever, and relaxed. Friends were safer than husbands and sisters, the damage they wrought less destructive.

'I have missed you so much.' *I just hadn't re-*

alised it. How dumb was that? Who forgot someone important in their lives because they'd fallen out about a man? Not any man, but Freddy. Luca had been right about him, but she wasn't going to acknowledge that. She couldn't bear to see the 'I told you so' sign flick on in his eyes again. Not yet anyway. Even if she could laugh because he'd won that argument there was too much pain behind it for her to be ready to make light of what had happened. That day would probably never come. 'We should never have stopped texting or emailing even when we were in different cities, no matter what we thought about what the other was doing.'

Luca swung her around in a circle, her feet nearly taking out the bed and then the chair with Chi sitting on it. 'I do solemnly swear never to stop annoying the hell out of my best buddy, Ellie, ever again.'

'Look out.' Chi leaped on top of the chair out of the way of Ellie's legs. 'Ellie makes you crazy, Luca.'

Ellie was put back on her feet and then Luca grabbed Chi and swung her in a circle. 'You're right, she does. I'd forgotten how to be crazy until today.'

Chi giggled and squirmed to be put down. 'Ellie, can I be your friend, too? I want to be crazy.'

'Absolutely. We'll be the three crazies.' Ellie reached for the girl and hugged her tight, trying hard not to let the lurking tears spill. What a day. What a damned amazing day. She'd found Luca, gained a new friend and was starting to feel a little bit like her old self. A teeny-weeny bit, but that was a start.

'Okay, crazies, time Ellie got ready to go out. Chi, I'm sorry but you're too young to go to a bar, but I'm sure we'll find somewhere else to take you while Ellie's here.' Luca cleared his throat and when Ellie looked up she'd swear there was moisture at the corners of his eyes, too.

It was all too much to cope with. Seeing Luca get all emotional wasn't helping her stay in control. 'Go on, shoo, both of you. I'm going to take another shower and get spruced up.'

'It's a bar in Vientiane, no need for glad rags.'

Luca grinned. Then slapped his forehead. 'Oh, I forgot. Lady El won't be seen anywhere in less than the best outfit.'

She picked up her pillow and threw it at him. 'Get out of here.'

She hadn't arrived in the best-looking outfit, even if she'd started out looking swanky back in Bangkok after a shower at the airport. But hey, in the interest of her self-esteem she wasn't going out in a sack, either. Though maybe here where the temperatures were so hot and the humidity high and everything definitely casual she could let go some of the debilitating need to be perfect. After all, there was no one here that she desperately had to please. Not even her friend. Luca had always accepted her for who she was, even if he did tease the hell out of her at times.

Suddenly she realised she was only dressed in a T-shirt and knickers; her bra lay on top of her discarded trousers. This might be Luca, but she had some pride. Glancing at him, she was dismayed to see his gaze was cruising down her body, hesitating on her breasts. She couldn't read the look in his eyes, but it was different from how he'd ever looked at her before.

Ellie shivered—with heat and apprehension. What was going on? 'Get out of here. I'll see you shortly.' She needed a shower, a very cold one.

'Like your dress,' Luca told her an hour later as she perched her backside on top of a high stool and leaned her elbow on the bar. 'When did you start wearing red?' His eyes held the same expression they had back in her room.

She chose to ignore it. 'Since I found the most amazing saleswoman in a very exclusive boutique.' It was true. That lady was very skilled at her job and her shop was Ellie's favourite, though lately there hadn't been any call for beautiful dresses.

The one she'd slipped into tonight was a simple sheath that was casual yet elegant. Her new look, she decided there and then. No more going for the tailored, exquisite clothes her husband had demanded she wear even to cook dinner. She'd miss the amazing clothes because she had loved them but hated the criticism rained down on her for not looking perfect enough. But, hey, she wasn't in that place anymore. She was with Luca in Vientiane. Ellie grinned. A real, deep all-or-nothing grin. Life was looking up. Strange glances from Luca or not.

'What's up? You look as if you won the lottery,' Luca pushed a glass of Beer Lao towards her.

The condensation on the glass made her mouth water and that was before she'd tasted the contents. 'As good as, I reckon. I'm starting to unwind and enjoy myself.'

'Things haven't been so great for you recently?' There was a guarded look in his eyes as though he was afraid of overstepping the mark. Something they'd never had to worry about in the past.

A deep gulp of beer and then, 'You were right. Freddy was an a-hole. I left him and now I'm trying to decide what it is I really want from my life.'

'I'm sorry to hear that.'

No gloating, thank goodness, or she'd have tipped her beer over his head. And that would've been such a waste. It was delicious. 'You know what? I'm not sorry.' It had only just occurred to her but, no, she was not sorry that episode of her life was over. Now all she had to do was pack it away completely. If that was possible consider-ing her sister's role in it. Hopefully, being so far removed from the complications of her family, she might find some inner peace. Though she might never learn to trust anyone after what had been done to her.

'Then, find that smile again.' Luca placed his hand on top of hers on the counter. 'You look better when your eyes light up with pleasure.'

Turning her hand over to clasp her fingers around his, she said, 'Seeing you makes me feel good. I couldn't believe it when you said my name.'

'*You* were surprised? I got a helluva shock con-sidering you weren't the doctor we were expect-ing. How was that for coincidence? Or was it our stars aligning or some such babble?'

'You've been here too long.' As laughter bub-bled up Ellie's throat something strange was going on with her hand. The one covered by

Luca's. She could feel heat and a zinging sensation that had nothing to do with the weather and all to do with— No way. She jerked her hand free, folded her arms across her chest and rubbed her arms vigorously.

'Ellie? You're going weird on me.' Luca locked his eyes on her.

Looking into those grey eyes, she searched for recognition of what had just happened but found nothing. Seemed her imagination was running riot. 'I'm fine,' she croaked.

'Phew. For a moment there I thought you were changing on me.' His gaze was intense, as if he was checking her out.

Zing. She felt it again. This time it was as if someone were lightly dancing down her spine. Tearing her eyes away from Luca, she snatched up her glass and drained the beer in one long gulp. The glass banged back on the counter and she stared around the bar, looking at everything and everyone but Luca.

'I'll get you another.' His hand scooped up her glass. The fingers that wrapped around the moist receptacle were long and strong, and tanned. Not that she understood why she was noticing.

Ellie's mouth dried, despite all the fluid she'd just swallowed. *They're only fingers. Luca's, what's more.* She shivered, as though it were cold, except the temperature was beyond high and her skin was on fire. What had just happened? She had to get herself under control. Getting wired over Luca was so not a good idea, let alone sensible. And despite her mistakes she was usually sensible. Or had that attribute flown out of the door and floated away on the Mekong just across the road?

Guess it had been so long since she'd been close to any man that her body had reacted without thought. But this was Luca. *Down, girl, down.* He was the last man on earth she should be having feelings about that had nothing to do with friendship and all to do with sex.

CHAPTER THREE

LUCA AIMED FOR relaxed, trying to ignore that something big was bugging Ellie. The defining strength of their friendship had taken a battering years back and he wasn't prepared to push. Not yet anyway. He'd hate to lose her now he'd just found her again. Not that he'd been looking. He'd kind of shut off most things from his previous life, except the mantra he'd always lived by— Chirsky men were bad husbands and fathers.

'I should head back to the compound,' Ellie muttered.

What happened to spending the evening together? 'Let's have another beer and then we'll eat.' Not waiting for her to answer, he waved at the barman busy with another order and indicated their empty glasses. He didn't want to walk even a few metres down the bar because

Ellie looked as if she was about to bolt, and that was the last thing he wanted.

He went with, 'It's unbelievable. I was coming into that room to meet some doctor I'd never heard of and there you were, looking like my Ellie.'

She blanched. Then slowly she slipped off the stool, standing straight—and bewildered. 'I really should go.' There was a wobble in her voice.

Luca placed a hand firmly on her shoulder. 'Sit down. The heat and travel hits you hard at first, but you need to stay awake till a reasonable hour to get your body clock back on track. The sooner the better.' He doubted those were the reasons for her looking as if she'd been run down by a train, but he played along. 'When I first arrived it took me ages to settle into a routine.'

'How long have you been here?' She still looked ready to flee.

'Nine months, three to go.'

Leaning her elbow on the counter, she propped her chin in her hand. 'Then what?'

'Maybe a spell in Cambodia.' Or Vietnam, or even Australia at a major hospital. He hadn't made any decisions about a whole load of things that involved his future since he'd come over here. He was avoiding them, because it was easier that way.

Her eyes widened and at last she gave him a smile. There were long gaps between those and he was already learning to appreciate them. She asked, 'Since when did you want to give up your goal of being head of the busiest A and E department in New Zealand?'

The problem with changing the subject so Ellie would relax was that he ended up in the hot seat. About to start telling her about the clinic's pet pangolin instead, he paused. They used to tell each other just about everything. Shouldn't he start renewing their friendship by doing what they'd always done? 'Gaylene doing her little number on me was a shock.' *That's an understatement, El, in case you don't realise.* 'I thought I'd made myself invulnerable, invincible, so that no one would catch me out. How wrong could a guy be? Maybe I'd become arrogant. I don't know.' He glanced across at Ellie and smiled despite himself. 'Okay, I was.' Hopefully that had changed. He'd sure as hell been taken down a peg or three, though not for anything to do with his medical work.

'I can understand wanting to protect your feelings but you're sounding as if you don't ever want to let anyone near, into your heart.' She eased her butt back onto the stool.

Luca felt some of the tension in his belly lighten. At least she didn't look quite so ready to run for the door anymore, but did she have to go straight to the centre of his problem? So easily? Maybe he hadn't missed her as much as he'd thought. But of course he had. Strange how he hadn't known that until he'd found her again. Should've done something about looking her up years ago, but he couldn't stand Baldwin. Not at all. 'I've never made any bones about the fact I do not want a family—no wife, no children.' Okay, *want* was the wrong word. He wouldn't risk having a wife and family. That was closer to the truth.

'That was an excuse for bonking every moving female while you were young, but not forever, surely?' She was laughing at him, soft and friendly-like but laughing nonetheless.

'Wrong,' he snapped. Telling her what made him who he'd become was a mistake after all. But then he'd known that, had always kept certain things to himself, even from this woman.

'Hey.' Her hand covered his. 'I didn't mean to upset you. You've got to admit you spent a lot of time chasing females back then.'

'I didn't have to chase anyone.' Yep, maybe he still was a little bit arrogant. A sigh huffed across his lips. 'You want to hear my story or not?'

The surprise in her eyes told him she hadn't expected him to continue his tale. *Well, Ellie, nor did I.* But now he'd started he didn't want to stop. He wanted her to know what drove him and how he'd arrived here. The idea of opening his heart to her appealed, when it had never done so in the past. Never. Which should be a warning.

So he stalled. 'Let's order some food. Want me to choose? Anything you won't like?'

'As I have no idea what the locals eat, you go ahead. I can't think of anything I won't enjoy. Tell you what, though, they brew great beer.'

'Their food's just as good.' He beckoned to the waitress and rattled off a few dishes he thought would be a good introduction to Lao food. Then he drank deeply from his glass and wiped the back of his hand over his mouth. 'My father left before we were born.' Ellie had met Angelique, his twin, when they were sharing that house in Auckland. Ange would often drop in for a night, sleeping on the floor in the corner of the lounge. 'Growing up knowing he'd never wanted to meet us, to be a part of our lives, that he didn't love us…' He paused, looked directly at Ellie. 'It was horrible. I used to look at men who were about the age I thought my father might be and wonder if they were our dad.'

Ellie ran her fingers down his arm. 'That's horrid. Did you never try to track him down through phone directories or electoral rolls when you were older?'

'Mum refused to tell us his name or where he came from, not even what he did for a living. Nothing. It was as though he'd never existed.'

'Her way of coping, maybe?'

'Possibly, but as kids we didn't understand

that. Hell, as an adult I still find it hard to accept.' He wasn't admitting to the equally awful thought that maybe his mother hadn't known who their father was because she'd slept with more than one man at the time they were conceived. As Gaylene had done with him, but they hadn't been a couple until she'd learned she was pregnant.

As far as his mum was concerned, he wouldn't judge her. His mother's life hadn't been easy growing up. Her father had been a bully and a thug to both her and her mother, and was not the kind of man a daughter could rely on for love and safety.

Understanding was blinking out at him from those hazel eyes less than a metre away. 'So when Gaylene declared you were the father of her baby you stepped up because no child of yours would not know their father.'

'Got it in one. Not that Gaylene knew my story, but she sure went for the jugular. In her eyes it didn't hurt that I was destined to become that head of department I'd planned on and would be earning a fat salary when I got there.' He tasted the sourness in his mouth. Thought he was long past letting what she'd done hurt him, huh? Thank goodness he hadn't loved her. That would've really turned him beyond bitter.

'You'd have married someone you didn't love for your child? Wouldn't it have been better for everyone to have remained single but fully involved with that child?' Ellie made everything seem so simple. Was that how she looked at life? A memory rose of her spitting words in his face, defending Baldwin when he'd tried to make her see reality. *He's a real man, of course he's played the field, but now he's settling down—with me,* she'd insisted.

Now she was here, without a wedding ring on her finger, and a change of name. Not so simple, eh?

'Didn't matter in the end,' he sighed. It hadn't been as straightforward as Ellie made it sound. Certainly not when Gaylene had been pressuring him so hard. He hadn't wanted to appear not to be taking his responsibilities seriously but at the same time it hadn't been easy to accept he was going to be a father when he'd spent his adult life doing his damnedest not to become one. 'I would never put any child through what Angelique and I had to deal with. Never.' Which was why he wasn't going to have children. Not only hadn't he known his father, his grandfather had been the worst example of a parent. He'd often wondered if having bad male role models on both sides of his family meant he'd be a terrible father, had inherited some chromosome that made men bad. He wasn't going to find out because if he was like them then it would be too late for any offspring he procreated.

'Oh, Luca, I never knew.' She locked those eyes on his. 'Not that I was meant to. I get that, too. But for the record I think you'd be a wonderful father. Just in case...' Her words trailed off.

Had the bile rising in his throat been that obvious? 'Thanks for the vote of confidence. It's good to know someone believes in me so blindly.'

'Ouch. You're not playing fair. I know you, have seen you working with children when they're in pain and terrified, still remember you cuddling Angelique's wee boy only hours after he was born. You have the right instincts, believe me.' This time she sipped her beer.

He'd like nothing more than to believe her, but that would be a huge leap of faith, right off the edge of the planet, in fact. He settled with, 'Wee Johnny is now at school and whipping up merry hell with his teachers. He wants to be an All Black without having to go through the usual channels.' Johnny was a great kid, so bright and busy and full of beans. He missed him.

'Is he? Got a photo?' Ellie seemed keen to get away from the uncomfortable conversation they'd been having.

He tugged his phone from the back pocket of his pants and tapped the icons. 'There. Isn't he a handsome dude?'

Snatching the phone from his grasp, Ellie stared at the picture. 'Just like his uncle.'

'I'm handsome?'

'I meant cheeky and obviously up to mischief.' She swiped the screen, moving on to more photos of his nephew. And Angelique. 'Oh. Your sister looks so much like your mother now.'

As in sad and bitter? 'Yes, the spitting image.' In every way. 'I tried to make up for Johnny not having a father, but for her I can't be anything but a brother.' Not even a good one now. Anger welled up. 'How could she have done the same thing as Mum? She knew what it was like not having a dad around the place. Hated it, and swore she'd never let her kids go unloved.'

'Hey.' Ellie's hand was back on his arm, warm and soft.

Almost sexy—if she wasn't a friend and that wasn't a friendly gesture. What was going on? Luca blinked. 'What?'

'Angelique's not as strong as you. Never was. Remember when you used to insist she should be studying at university for a career and she wanted to work in a café? She liked what she was doing, and you couldn't change who she was.'

'Yeah, I've finally worked that out.' *Focus, man. On the conversation and nothing else.* He had to be out of sorts because of Ellie's sudden reappearance in his life. He'd missed her. A lot. Yeah, that was all that odd sensation around her touch was about.

She hadn't finished. 'But, Luca, you support her, stand by her and look out for her son. That's huge.' Ellie sounded so sure, it was scary.

'Wrong. I'm over here, not at home, aren't I?' Guilt ramped up, but Angelique had told him to get out of her life and stop interfering with how she raised her son just about the time his carefully planned career was getting on top of him. It had begun to seem a hollow victory when there was no one to share it with. He'd started questioning everything he'd believed in. Except not being a parent. That was non-negotiable. No exceptions.

Hot spices wafted through the air and four small plates of mouth-watering food appeared on the counter in front of them. Perfect timing. This talking with Ellie was getting too deep and uncomfortable.

She was licking her lips and sniffing the air like a dog on the scent. He did what he always did when the going got tough—he grinned. Amazing how that helped all the tension fall away. However temporary, it felt good to be with her knowing she wouldn't try to rip him off or take something from him he didn't want to give. Good friends were rare and priceless. And El was the best. So why did he feel he had to keep reminding himself of that? It was as though something had changed between them that he couldn't fathom. Luca shrugged. He had four weeks to work it out before she headed home again.

The woman distracting him said, 'Tell me more about the clinic.'

A reprieve, then. 'It's heartbreaking seeing what these children deal with, and yet uplifting because of their sunny natures and how they take it all in their little strides.'

'I was really moved today when the kids gathered around me, all chatter and laughter when they'd never met me.' The sticky rice and peanut sauce were delicious. Ellie forked up more and watched Luca do the same. He'd told her more about his past tonight than in all the previous years she'd known him. He'd surprised her, but then today had been full of surprises on all fronts.

Thinking back, she saw where she'd missed

little clues about his past. Whenever talk had got around to families he'd been reticent, and she couldn't remember what he'd said about his father except he hadn't been around. Not once had he said that the man had never been there, was basically unknown. Hell, she might've got her marriage all wrong but her family had always been there for her when she was growing up. It was different nowadays, though. Awkward and sometimes downright hostile with Caitlin still coming and going in her parents' lives as though she'd done nothing wrong. But Luca had missed out on a lot, hadn't had that loving childhood she'd had, so why wasn't he wanting to have his own family and make up for that? Had he ever fallen in love? Come close, even? Sad, but she suspected not.

'Are you listening to me?' Luca elbowed her, causing rice to drop off her fork.

'Heard every word.' *I hope, or I'll be asking questions about what he's just told me tomorrow and then he'll give me stick.* 'The clinic is full to bursting at the moment.'

His grey eyes squinted at her. 'I said there are four spare beds.'

'You did not.' She laughed, and even to her that sounded strained. She changed the subject and determined to concentrate on everything he said. 'Who's Baxter?' She'd heard the kids talking about him when she was getting ready to come out with Luca.

'The clinic's pet pangolin.' She must've looked bewildered because he explained further. 'An anteater. They normally live in the trees. Apparently this one turned up one day with one leg half severed off. It was before my time. Aaron operated and now it slopes around minus a leg.'

'So Baxter knew where to go for an amputation.' This time her laughter was genuine.

Luca smiled back. 'The kids adopted him and he's stayed, sometimes foraging for ants farther afield, but he never goes very far. You'll see him soon enough.'

He pushed their empty plates aside. 'Feel up to a stroll beside the Mekong?'

Not really. She'd like nothing more than to fall into bed and get some more sleep. Glancing at her watch, she saw it was only just after eight thirty. And here she'd thought they'd been in the bar for hours. It was too early to go back to her room, especially after having slept most of the day. An evening stroll with Luca would be the next best thing. Maybe even better, and she could walk off the effects of all that beer. What had she been thinking having so much? Hadn't been thinking at all, that was what. Standing up, she slung her bag over her shoulder. 'Sure.'

Outside the air had cooled all of about two degrees. Ellie shook her head. 'To think I was looking forward to the warmth after a particularly cold spring back home.'

Luca caught her hand in his and swung their arms between them. 'I still haven't got used to the heat. Especially at night when I'm desperately tired and sleep's evasive.'

Ellie gently squeezed his hand, enjoying the strength of those firm fingers. This felt good. Being with someone who knew her and wouldn't make up things about her, wouldn't be sniggering behind her back, wouldn't be breaking any vows.

Neither of them talked as they strolled along a path lined with bars and nightclubs. Despite the noise from those buildings the sound of the river seeped into Ellie's mind, a steady pouring of an unbelievable amount of water carrying debris and fish along its path. Where had that branch come from? A few kilometres farther north? Or from another country? China, even? 'Amazing.'

'What is?'

'The river and all the countries it runs through.' Ellie turned towards Luca and missed her footing on the uneven surface.

He caught her waist, held her as she regained her balance. 'Careful. Can't have you breaking your ankle before you've even started working with us.'

'That would make me very unpopular.' Those hands were definitely showing their strength. And their heat. She could feel each finger distinctly from the others. A different kind of warmth than what the climate was producing caressed her feverish skin. Tipping her head back, she met Luca's stunned look. Carefully taking a backwards step, she extricated herself from his hold and dropped her gaze. And instantly felt she'd lost something. Something important. But this was Luca. Not some hot guy she'd want to go to bed with.

Really? Luca wasn't hot? Yes, he was, but she'd never thought of him like that. That would be too— Too strange? Or too hot to handle? She peeked up at him, found him staring out at the river now, an inscrutable look on his face. When had he got so good at those? Not back when she'd last knew him, for sure. Back then he used to make jokes to divert unwanted interest. These days she also had a few of her own special expressions that hadn't been around in those days.

'I think it's time for me to get back to my room,' she muttered and began to turn around.

'No problem.'

Even his voice sounded different: deeper, huskier. Reading way too much into everything? Eek, was she on the rebound from Freddy? The thought slammed into her brain, almost paralysing her. Was that what this was about? Reacting strangely to Luca because she felt safe with him? Could trust him? He'd never hurt her, physically or mentally. No, but she could get hurt by her own stupidity. Because she was being stupid. She mightn't have seen or spoken to Luca for years but she knew him—as a friend, and he was perfect like that. She didn't need or want to have anything else with him. Surely tomorrow she'd wake up refreshed and over whatever was ailing her.

'Ellie, are you all right?' His concern sounded genuine.

Had he not felt anything? Did that mean she could relax? No. Not until she'd stopped these silly sensations tripping her up every time Luca touched her. If she didn't, four weeks working with him were going to be tricky. Luca had always touched his friends whenever he wanted to share something with them or comfort them. 'I think I'm so tired I have no idea which way's up.' Which was completely true. 'I shouldn't have had those beers.'

'They might help you drop off to sleep quickly.'

He waved over a hovering taxi. 'Come on, Sleeping Beauty. Time for your bed.'

Huh? Sleeping Beauty? More like droopy sad sack.

Luca handed Ellie out of the taxi and paid the driver. 'I wish they wouldn't turn all the outside lights off,' he growled as they headed up the path to the staff sleeping quarters.

'I'd have trouble finding my room if you weren't with me,' Ellie agreed.

'You'll soon know your way around. It's not a complex setting. The hospital is at the back with long wings off three sides. Ours is on the right and houses staff quarters, wards and our small operating theatre, with the tourist centre at the very end.'

'Tourists?' In a medical centre?

'The museum room. There're photos of bombs in the ground and the craters caused when they explode. Pictures of wounded children and their families hang everywhere. There's a real bomb that's had the detonator removed in the centre of the main viewing room, which is very dramatic and has tourists putting their hands in their pockets for money to fix more kids. Not that we'd stop even if the funds were rock bottom.'

'Is the foundation struggling?' Ellie asked, thinking that she could easily hand back the money she was being paid for her month here. She felt sure she was going to be the winner of her time spent with these wonderful people. Money didn't compare to exchanging hugs with a thirteen-year-old with only one arm who was determined to become a teacher when he grew up, as one lad had told her in her first five minutes here.

'Struggling's probably a bit strong, but there's never a well of cash. The foundation relies heavily on donations. One benefactor in the States has set up an investment fund that pays handsome dividends, and without that I'd say we'd be in big trouble.' Luca spoke with authority, as though he'd dug deep to learn all he could about the organisation helping these kids. No surprises there.

'You are getting quite a kick out of working

in such a different environment from what you were used to, aren't you?'

'More than I'd expected,' Luca acknowledged. 'At first I worried I'd been stupid to sign up for twelve months, but it didn't take long to realise that I was enjoying practising medicine outside my usual comfort levels. There's as much drama here as in an A and E department, as you'll soon learn. But more than that, I'm in on the follow-up care, and over here that means getting to know the whole family—if there is a family, that is.' His voice went from excited to sad within a few words.

Ellie wrapped an arm around his waist. 'Reality sucks, doesn't it?'

'It can.' Then he said with what she thought was a smile in his voice, 'Then there are the success stories, like Chi who wants to become a doctor to help her people. She's going to Australia with Louise and Aaron when they decide to return home, which they're saying will be within two years.'

'What happens when they go? Are there replacements queuing to get in?'

He shrugged. 'Who knows?'

Was Luca considering it? 'Would you put your hand up?'

'The idea has crossed my mind.'

'You don't want to return home? You don't miss Auckland?' Now that they'd reconnected she didn't want to lose him again, but that didn't mean she'd be moving over here full time so as to spend more time with him.

Going back to the city where she'd done her internship and had loads of good times with Luca and her housemates had been an obvious choice when the temporary position at Auckland Hospital became available. She'd be housesitting for the specialist she was covering for and couldn't move into the house until he and his family headed away to America for his sabbatical.

A part of her still wanted the house-and-kids package—with a hot man, of course. But that meant learning to trust again, and she wasn't brimming with confidence of that happening. Especially since it wasn't only her husband who'd cheated on her but her sister, as well.

Sometimes she thought Caitlin's treachery was worse. They'd been so close. *Not close enough to see she loved your husband.* True. Caitlin and Freddy were apparently talking about getting married when the divorce was settled. They had a wait on their hands because with New Zealand law that couldn't happen for more than another year.

Luca twisted out of her hold, reminding her he was with her. He'd remained silent for so long her mind had taken a trip into things she didn't need to be thinking about right now. Had her question about missing home hit a chord? Should she press the point? Once she would've. But there were years between then and now. She went for the easy option. 'You've gone quiet on me.'

'I don't have a home to miss. Angelique and Johnny have their own lives to lead that apparently don't include me. Auckland is my hometown, always will be, but it'll be there whenever I choose to return.'

'Hell, Luca.' That sounded incredibly sad and bleak. Where was the man who was always happy and making jokes, always acting as though he didn't have a worry in the world? Had he been leading a double life? But then she hadn't known about his father, or lack of one, until tonight, either. She stopped to look up at him, only just seeing his facial expressions in the star-studded darkness. The sadness for him grew into something else, roiling through her so that she wanted to reach out and touch him deeply, to show he wasn't alone, that she cared. 'I will never let you out of my life again.'

His jaw moved as he swallowed. He was staring at her, his eyes unblinking. When he spoke his voice was low and loaded with emotion. 'Thank goodness for that. It's been too long, El.'

Way too long, and the worst thing was that she hadn't even noticed until today. Reaching out to him, she was going to hug him, as she used to whenever they'd celebrated an exam pass or lost a patient or felt a little lonely. But then Luca's arms were tugging her in against his body, his head dipping so that his mouth found hers. With his lips on hers, his tongue slipped inside her mouth.

Ellie breathed deep, drew in Luca, a mix of beer and chilli and hot male. Of safety and—hot male. Surrendering to the need clawing through her, she focused on kissing him back and hoping she was wiping away that sadness that had been rolling off him in waves.

Then as suddenly as it started, the kiss ended. Luca abruptly dropped his arms and stumbled backwards. 'Ellie, I'm so sorry. I don't know what came over me. Look, that door to our right is your room. I'll see you tomorrow.' And he was gone, racing back the way they'd come, out onto the road and still he didn't slow down.

'Thanks very much, Luca. You're sorry? Talk about taking a knife and cutting into me. You're sorry for a mind-blowing kiss that I reckon you were enjoying as much as I was?'

But she was talking to the night. Luca was way beyond hearing her. Staring around the dark grounds, she could only sigh with relief that the lights were out. Doubtful anyone had seen them kissing. But her heart wasn't letting her off that easily. It pounded hard and fast while her hands shook and her skin tightened with need. Luca. What had they done? Whatever it was, she wasn't sorry. But she should be. She'd been kissing the man when only minutes before she'd acknowledged she never wanted to let him out of her life again. *Way to go, Ellie. No one kisses a friend like that, with that intensity and emotion.* It was sexy; very, very sexy. And her body was suffering withdrawal already. Which meant the future of their friendship was now in jeopardy.

CHAPTER FOUR

LUCA STUMBLED ALONG the road, not bothering to look where he was going. What had he been thinking when he'd kissed Ellie? He hadn't been thinking. That was the problem. Not with his brain anyhow. Ellie, of all people. He'd kissed her, his best friend, damn it.

And wanted to do it again.

No, I don't.

Yes, he did. Now. Sooner than later.

Oaths rent the air blue. What had he done to their friendship? As if that was going to move ahead after that particular little fiasco. Damn it. Ellie was—El. His long-lost friend. So lost he'd have been able to get in touch with her simply by going online and looking up her phone number. Or ringing the A and E department at Wellington Hospital. But he hadn't done it. He'd been smarting over her telling him to butt out of her life if he wasn't prepared to accept her decision to marry the man who was now her ex. Being right felt hollow. He regretted walking away. Not even being preoccupied with his own problem in a short skirt was an excuse. He'd let Ellie down.

Ellie didn't ring you, either.

Didn't make it right. But nor was kissing her right. It had to be way up there with the dumbest things he'd ever done in his whole goddamned life. Worse, they had to work together for four whole weeks. That could prove uncomfortable. Or interesting.

Come up with some good news, will you?

Nope, couldn't think of any at this moment.

His pace slowed and he jammed his fists on his hips, tipped his head back to stare up at the sky.

No answers up there.

He resumed walking at a slower pace, breathing deep, letting the heavy, warm air calm him. There were no answers at all. He'd spent an evening talking with Ellie, sometimes about subjects they'd never touched on before, like about his sorry past. He'd got tied up in the fun of seeing her again and spilled his guts. Then he'd goddamned kissed her.

He needed his head read—only problem there it was such a shambles no one would be able to make anything out of it.

It was some kiss, though.

Shut up.

Go on. Admit it. When did a kiss ever give you an achy feeling in your heart?

There was the answer he was looking for. He hadn't realised just how much he'd missed Ellie, and now his heart was happy. As in how one friend would feel about another after four years' absence and everything that had happened in that time. For Ellie that had been a failed marriage for reasons he had yet to find out, and for him the loss of a child he'd never wanted but hated the opportunity being stolen from him. But Gaylene had only started this sense of not belonging anywhere. Angelique with her outrageous demands that he stay out of her and Johnny's lives had exacerbated his need to question everything he'd thought *his* life was about. Including being the head of a large A and E department.

No wonder his emotions were all over the show. That kiss had come out of nowhere, blindsiding him. Now all he had to do was move on and forget it ever happened.

Yep, that should work. Easy as.

Ellie woke slowly the next morning, her head feeling as though fog had slipped in to fill it while she'd been comatose. Guess the good news was that she'd slept at all. After Luca's knee-knocking, bone-rattling kiss she'd figured she'd never sleep again.

Luca had been late getting in last night. She'd heard him bumping into furniture in the next-door bedroom that she knew was his. Had he gone back to town and found a bar to try to drown out that kiss? Or didn't he care that he'd kissed her and stirred up all sorts of emotions she so wasn't ready to deal with?

Knock, knock.

'Who is it?' *Please don't be Luca.* Not yet

while she was still in her satin shorts and cotton top.

'It's Chi. You've got to get up. Breakfast's nearly ready.'

Phew. Sometimes she did get what she asked for. 'Come in, Chi.'

The girl opened the door cautiously and peered around the room before stepping inside and closing the door again. 'Morning, Ellie. You've had a big sleep.'

If only that were true. A certain someone and his kiss had kept her awake staring into the dark for hours until eventually exhaustion had won out and dragged her under for a brief spell. 'I don't know where the kitchen is yet. Do you want to show me around after I get dressed?'

Chi nodded solemnly. 'We have breakfast early before everyone begins working. Then the tourists start visiting at nine.'

'Right. I'm heading for the shower. Two minutes, okay?' She snatched some clothes from her bag that had yet to be unpacked.

Chi was still in Ellie's room when she returned from a fast and cold shower. The bed had been made, every corner tucked in neatly, the pillow perfectly straight and the cover smoothed so as not one wrinkle showed.

'Thank you so much, but you don't have to look after me. I'm sure there are lots of other people here who need you more than me.'

'I like you.'

Tears blocked Ellie's throat. A hug was called for. It was the only way she could show her feelings right now with words backing up behind the lump in her throat, unable to squeeze past. For everything this child must've suffered it all came down to simple observations and reactions. Give and take. Hugs. 'I like you, too,' she finally managed to get out, then focused on getting ready for the day. She slapped on some make-up. Even here she'd try to look her best.

Not for Luca by any chance? *No way.*

'You've got a text.' Chi nodded at her phone on the desk.

Probably Mum or Dad. Despite the rift between her and Caitlin that overlapped into her relationship with her parents they would still want to know how she was settling in. Then another thought snapped into her head. What if it was from Luca?

'Come on, Chi, show me where to go.'

If it was from Luca he could wait until she'd worked out how to handle today after what went down last night.

She couldn't resist. Snatching up the phone as she headed out, she pressed Messages and gasped. It was from her sister, Caitlin. There was nothing she wanted to hear from her. Her finger hovered over the delete button. What if something had happened to Mum or Dad? That would be a good enough reason for Caitlin to text. But wouldn't she ring if that was the case?

She sighed. The message read, Just checking to see you arrived safe and sound.

Why don't you ask Mum? I sent them a message on the way in from the train station.

Ellie shoved the phone into her shorts pocket and followed Chi. What was Caitlin up to now? They didn't do texts or any form of communicating. That had finished the day she'd learned the truth about her sister and her husband. It had been a stunning birthday present; one she'd never forget. But sometimes when she wasn't thinking clearly she did admit to missing Caitlin. They'd been closer than grapes in a bunch, told each other everything. Everything? As in 'I'm sleeping with your husband, Ellie,' everything?

'In here.' Chi took her hand to tug her into a long narrow room that housed the kitchen and a very long trestle table.

'You must be Ellie.' A man in his late forties and of average height crossed the room, his hand extended in greeting. 'I'm Aaron. Sorry for the confusion yesterday about who you were. I've been in touch with headquarters and they admitted the oversight was entirely their fault.'

Ellie shook his hand in return. 'It doesn't matter. I'm here, you've got the bases covered. That's what's important.'

'True. We'll try to break you in quietly today. But there's no telling what will come in the doors at any given moment.' Aaron's smile was completely guileless and relaxed Ellie enough to put her sister aside for a more appropriate time when she was on her own.

Her nose twitched as the smell of something

hot and delicious reached her. 'What do we eat for breakfast?'

'*Chew makork*. Eggs, carrots and sticky rice,' Chi told her.

Different. 'Bring it on.'

It was simple and delicious. There were other vegetables with the carrots, and a chilli sauce made her skin heat and her mouth water. For her the food was all part of the adventure.

Unfortunately so was the grim awakening as to why she was here that arrived as everyone was finishing breakfast.

Aaron, who'd headed away to check on a patient he'd operated on yesterday, now stood in the doorway. 'Incoming patients. Two of them. All hands on deck. Ellie, that includes you. We'll show you the ropes as we go along.'

Gulp. She hadn't seen the hospital or the small theatre yet. 'I'm ready.' *Fake it till you make it*. It wasn't as though she didn't know what to do, but she'd have liked a few minutes to learn where everything was kept.

Louise must've seen her hesitation because she said, 'You'll be fine.'

Love it when people who know next to nothing about you except what was in your CV say that. Ellie shook her head and prepared to face whatever had arrived in the little building at the end of the garden. 'Where's Luca this morning?'

His absence had surprised her. Was he avoiding her? That would be plain silly considering they had to spend a lot of time together over the next few weeks. Better to front up to last night and move on.

'He went out early to visit a family in a village who don't have the wherewithal to get in here for check-ups and dressing changes. It happens a lot and we try to accommodate everyone.'

Maybe he hadn't gone to get away from her. Ellie wasn't sure how she felt about Luca this morning. Good, bad or indifferent? Certainly not indifferent. Or bad. Okay, so her feelings were good. As in friends good? Or more? As in used to be friends, now might be something else? Lovers? Well, there wasn't anything else. She wasn't going down the full-blown relationship of being married and contemplating kids track for a long time—if at all. Her skin prickled with the humiliation of her last attempt at that. Then there was the pain she'd known as all her dreams had shrivelled up into a dry heap.

'In here.' Louise turned into a large room busy with people dashing back and forth and someone crying out in agony.

The sight had Ellie drawing on all her strength not to gasp out loud. The young patient being carried across the room hadn't had the benefit of an ambulance crew and a relatively soft ride. The child had been piggybacked in by a small man, the blood from where a foot should've been dripping a trail right across the hospital room. At least someone had managed to tie a make-shift tourniquet around his lower thigh so that the blood flow had been minimised, though not completely stopped.

'Where's the other patient?' she asked, try-ing not to convey her horror as she and Louise lifted the unconscious boy off the man's back and placed him on a bed. 'Aaron said patients, plural.'

'In front of us. The boy's father. He has an in-jury to his buttocks.' Louise nodded at a gaping wound that Ellie hadn't noticed as she'd been too busy focusing on the child. 'You can take him over to that bed for an assessment and report back to Aaron. Noi will interpret for you.'

'I haven't met Noi yet,' Ellie said over her shoulder as she approached her patient.

Louise beckoned a young man over and made the introductions. 'Noi learned English at school. He wants to be a doctor and is spending time with us until he can get into medical school here in Vientiane.'

'*Sabaai dii.*' She'd learned the greeting that morning over sticky rice and carrots. 'Lovely to meet you.' Ellie shook Noi's hand.

The way Noi said *sabaai dii* was definitely an improvement on her botched attempt.

She smiled. 'I need practice.'

Noi nodded. 'You'll soon learn. Let's help the father.'

Ellie could not imagine how the man they were easing onto the bed had carried his son on his back with the wound she was now seeing. He'd have been in agony, even without the constant pummelling he'd received from his load, yet he hadn't said a word or groaned out loud. Turning to Noi, she said, 'Can you explain to our patient what I'm going to do? Also ask if he has any other injuries.'

While Noi spoke rapidly in Laotian she cut away what was left of the man's trousers, careful to be as discreet as possible, and hearing the tremor in the father's voice as he replied to Noi.

Noi told her, 'The father heard the explosion and found his son on the side of the road with his foot missing. When he stepped around him to lift him away from the danger another, smaller explosion happened. That's when he was hurt.'

Lucky for him there were no other injuries. This one was bad enough and going to cause him a lot of pain and anguish until it mended.

Crossing to where Louise and Aaron were working on the boy, she reported, 'That wound on the buttocks is the only injury. Muscle damage is severe and will require deep suturing. I need to administer pain relief before cleaning the wound and stitching.'

Aaron replied, 'Louise will get what you require from the drugs cabinet. Later this morning when we're done with these patients I'll show you everything and give you the codes for that and other locked rooms.'

'We'll be in surgery shortly with this lad, trying to save his lower leg,' Louise told her. 'Can you intubate him while I get what you require?'

'Of course.' She swapped places with Louise, and suctioned the lad's airway clear of fluids prior to inserting the tube. Next she attached the mask and began running oxygen, keeping an eagle eye on the boy's breathing. 'Don't the locals know to stay clear of the bombs? Or am I being simplistic?'

Aaron was having difficulty getting a needle into a vein in the thin forearm but eventually managed to get it into a vein on the back of the boy's hand, giving access for saline and drugs. 'At last.' He looked up at Ellie. 'You're seeing things as someone coming from a safe and relatively comfortable society does, as we've all done when we first arrived. These people are extremely poor. Scrap metal fetches on the market what's to them a lot of money. If a child can sell a piece he's helping feed his family. It's a no-brainer for them. It's also why a lot of children are missing limbs. Or worse. Welcome to Laos.'

Ellie surprised herself by finding a smile. 'I'm glad to be here. Truly.' Helping people and animals when they were in need had always been a big deal to her, and was the reason she'd gone into medicine. At first she'd been aiming to become a vet, but as she'd got older she'd swapped frogs and guinea pigs for humans. The idea of going to vet school had been quickly vanquished when her favourite dog had to be put down after being run over by a truck. No way could she ever deliberately put down any living creature, even if it was for the best. She just didn't have what it took.

Louise returned and handed her a kidney dish containing vials and syringes. 'Here you go. Once you've finished there can you move over to the day clinic and help with the day patients? I'm sorry we haven't had time to show you the ropes, but Luca assures us you're very good at your job.'

Luca had? Guess he'd talked with these two about her yesterday while she'd been in dreamland. He was four years out of touch, but she'd take the compliment anyway. Those had been lacking lately, and it felt good to have someone still believing in her without qualification. 'Not a problem.'

'Thanks.' Louise began heading for Theatre, then paused. 'If Luca's not back when you're ready, ask Noi to introduce you to everyone.'

'Here I go, then,' Ellie whispered as she vigorously scrubbed her hands under a tap. 'The first day of a new venture. The first day after Luca kissed me.' And apparently he was due back any time soon. How would they look each other in the eye? The knowledge of their responses to that kiss had to come between them. So how to move beyond it without making a hash of things? If they didn't, the rest of her days here would be uncomfortable and difficult for both of them.

Ellie, focus on the job and stop worrying about the tomorrows.

If only it were that easy.

It could be. Face it, why did everything have

to be complicated? What would be wrong about having a few kisses with Luca? Seeing where they led? Chances were they'd get over each other quickly and return to a relationship they were comfortable with. Not one where they didn't see each other or talk together for years, please. She was done with that. Done with losing the people in her life that were precious to her. Getting one person back was amazing, and she needed to tread carefully or risk losing him again.

So how did one go about retracting a kiss?

A memory of the heat that had zapped between them at his touch told her. It was impossible. As in it was too late. She was fried. The chances of looking at Luca without wondering what it would be like to feel his body against hers, inside her, were remote. This rebound thing had a lot to answer for. Who'd have thought it? The only explanation she could come up with on the spot was that she knew Luca well and would be safe with him while she tried to find her feet in the dating game. But she hadn't been contemplating getting into that murky pool for some time to come.

* * *

Luca leaned a shoulder against the door frame of the outpatients' clinic. A yawn rolled up and out, stretching his mouth and making him aware of the grit in his eyes. Damn, he was tired. Sleep had been impossible last night. Every time he'd closed his eyes his mind had filled with images of Ellie.

Ellie blinking at him in astonishment as he'd crossed the room to hug her for the first time in years.

Ellie in that curve-hugging shift dress that emphasised her figure and did nothing to curb the desire tugging at his manhood.

Ellie looking glum when she mentioned her broken marriage. Not that she'd said a lot. But there'd definitely been sadness and despair in those hazel pools that seemed to draw him in deeper every time he locked gazes with her. Like a vortex, swirling faster and faster. He had yet to hit the centre, but it was coming. He could feel it in his muscles—each and every one of them, damn it.

Watching her now as she talked to Noi, obviously getting him to explain to their patient what she had to do to help him, Luca felt that peculiar clenching of his heart again. A sensation he'd only felt once before—yesterday when he'd been with Ellie.

So much for heading out early to avoid her until he'd got his thoughts and emotions into some semblance of order. Only minutes back at the clinic and he was in trouble. Wondering where these feelings would lead him. Hoping nothing was about to come between him and Ellie again. He'd do anything for that not to happen.

So he wouldn't be kissing her again?

Damn right he wouldn't.

Dragging air deep into his lungs, he crossed to help with her patient. 'Hey, need a hand?'

Startled eyes locked on him. 'Luca. When did you get back?'

'Minutes ago.' There were green flecks in her eyes he hadn't noticed before. Could eyes change like that? Or had he just opened his wider? Begun to see things that had always been before him? 'What's the story here?' He tried to shut down the runaway heat speeding through his veins. 'Apart from those buttocks, I mean.'

'Nothing else. This man's been lucky.' Ellie's mouth twisted. 'I mean luckier than his son, and luckier than he might've been. It's unbelievable what's happened to them.'

Touching a finger to the back of her hand, Luca nodded. 'It's okay. I know what you mean. It takes time to get past the horror of bombs blowing up and hurting innocent people. This is for real, and we are so not used to it. You'll never get comfortable with it to the point you stop thinking and wondering why it has to happen at all, but you will come to accept that it does and we're here to help.'

Her teeth nibbled at her bottom lip as she stared down at the wound she was about to repair. 'Thanks. I needed to hear that. Here I was thinking I'd seen it all in the emergency department. Stabbings, shootings, high-speed car crashes. Awful scenarios, but this—' she waved a hand through the air '—children, adults, bombs, severed limbs. It's grotesque.'

'Yes, it is. Now, do you want me to assist while you put this man back together?' One of the nurses could do that but he was hoping with everything he had she'd say yes. He wanted to work with her. Maybe then reality would return, banishing this stupid need thickening his blood every time he so much as looked at Ellie. Time spent doing a medical procedure together would bring back memories of their training days in A and E and hopefully follow on with more reminders of what their relationship was about.

'That would be great,' she answered. 'I've given him painkillers, enough that hopefully he'll be drowsy while I stitch him back together.' Ellie proceeded to outline how she intended going about fixing her patient's wound. 'What happens when we've patched him up? Does he stay here?'

Luca shook his head. 'He will be transferred to Mahosot Hospital. We don't keep adult patients in our ward.'

The man turned his head to stare at Luca. He asked in Laotian, 'My boy. Where is he? Is he safe?'

When Luca interpreted Ellie told him, 'Aaron has him in Theatre. He's lost his foot and ankle.

You'll know what to tell him about how Aaron will help his boy.'

Nodding, Luca explained to the father how the doctors would clean the stump and stop the blood flow. He kept it brief and simple. There'd be time later for the family to come to terms with the extent of the surgery going on in Theatre. Then he focused on assisting Ellie.

They worked well together, each anticipating the other's requirements without a word being spoken. And yes, the memories flooded in, unnerving him. A whiff of the past when they worked well together gave a hint of what the future could hold if they went down that track.

Nearly thirty minutes later Ellie tied off the last stitch and reached for a swab to clean the last of the blood on the surrounding skin. 'The risk of infection will be high, especially if this man goes back to his village in the next few days. What's the next step in his treatment?'

'Don't expect him to stay in hospital. There'll be pressing issues back home he'll want to attend to, like earning enough money for food,' Luca told her.

'The people I saw sitting on the front step yesterday when I arrived. They were parents of our patients?' She added, 'I thought *they* were the patients.'

'They'd mostly be mums and dads.'

'What about our man's son? Will he go home, too?' Again horror was reflected in her eyes.

A gnawing need to hold her tight against him and to shield her from all this grew larger and larger, and he had to swallow hard to hold back. 'Hopefully, with Noi's help, we can persuade the family to leave the boy with us until his wound heals. Sometimes a relative will move in to be with their family member, but that depends on if they can afford someone to be away from home for so long.'

'I've lived a very sheltered life.' Ellie lifted sad eyes to him.

'You're not regretting coming here?' He hoped not. Otherwise her month would stretch out interminably for her. But he also didn't want her stressed by what she was dealing with. Not everyone could cope with it, and Ellie seemed to already be under pressure from something else.

'Not at all. It's an eye-opener and I think I needed that. I've been getting too self-absorbed lately.'

Guess a marriage breakup might do that. 'Come on, we'll grab a coffee while we can. Day clinic starts shortly. I'll be showing you the ropes.'

And working my tail off to forget that damned kiss.

'What do you do for a social life here?' Ellie asked, her eyes not quite meeting his.

'Drink beer with long-lost friends,' he answered flippantly.

'That exciting, eh?'

'Yeah, very exciting.'

'Luca, about last night—'

He shouldn't have said *very exciting*. She was getting the wrong idea. 'Last night was a mistake, okay? I'm putting it down to the shock and surprise of us catching up when we least expected it. Nothing more than that.'

'Fine.' Her gaze dropped, focused somewhere below his chin. 'That's good. I'll do that, too.'

Yeah, except it didn't feel good. Not at all.

CHAPTER FIVE

In Outpatients, Ellie ruffled a toddler's hair while squatting down beside the wee tot to check out a healing wound on the girl's arm. Luca's mouth dried. Ellie was beautiful. More beautiful than ever, even with that wariness that never seemed to completely go away. How could he not have kept in touch? Even knowing that the man she'd chosen to marry was wrong for her, especially knowing that, he should never have let other things get in the way of their friendship.

But he had. Now she was back, in his life, on his turf. And he was having these weird and wonderful reactions to her. Weird and wonderful? Or weird and weirder?

Beside him Noi said, 'The children already love her.'

'She certainly has a way with them,' Luca acknowledged. Not something he'd particularly noticed before. But then why would he? He hadn't been in the habit of taking notes of her attributes.

As Ellie carefully lifted the toddler's shirt she spoke softly and got no resistance to her gentle prods around the child's rib cage.

Luca sighed. 'She'd make a wonderful mother.'

He hadn't realised he'd spoken out loud until Noi asked, 'Ellie doesn't have children already?'

'In the Western world it's not uncommon for women to have children later in life than they do here.' Did Ellie want children of her own? He couldn't remember ever discussing that with her, but then they'd been so busy getting on with becoming doctors they hadn't been looking that far ahead. Until she'd met Baldwin, that was.

Noi shook his head, but refrained from comment. Probably didn't understand the differences between their cultures. 'I'll see you in the ward.'

'Luca, there you are,' a little boy squealed and ran across the room to him.

Ellie jerked around, a startled look on her face. 'Luca.' She gave him a brief nod and returned to her patient.

As he reached for the boy flinging himself at

him he winced. Ellie hadn't been falling over herself to be friendly since yesterday when they'd talked about their kiss. While he should be grateful she wasn't pushing for a follow-up kiss, a part of him wished otherwise. He'd like nothing more than to repeat it, to taste her sweetness again, to feel his body fire up in anticipation of something more. No, not that. That desire had kept him awake again last night. Keep this up and he'd be a walking zombie by the time her month was up.

'Luca, say hello,' the boy demanded.

'Hi, Pak. How's that arm?' he asked, watching Ellie and tucking the boy against his chest.

'It's better now. The concrete can come off.'

'No, it can't. You've got another week before I remove it.'

A smile was hovering at the corners of Ellie's mouth, as though afraid to come out fully. 'Concrete, eh?'

'It's what the kids call their casts. Concrete sleeves,' he explained as Pak wriggled in his arms. 'You want to get down already?' he asked in Laotian.

'Yes.'

'I like that you speak the lingo.' Ellie stood up, admiration lightening those big eyes and lifting her mouth into a full, delicious smile.

Delicious smile? He was deranged. Had to be. Why else was he wanting to kiss that mouth? Again? When he knew absolutely that it would be wrong, would lead to all sorts of complications? 'Not very well.'

The smile faltered, disappeared. 'You've made a start.' She turned away, picked up a stethoscope and knelt down to the toddler, who seemed rooted to the floor as she stared at Ellie. Had she fallen for her, too?

Fallen for her? *No damned way. I have not.* This was getting stranger and stranger. Luca mentally slapped his head. Put Pak down. Strode back the way he'd come, heading for the ward and the children who needed him to check their stumps, needed encouragement to start walking again, or using arms that were shorter than they used to be. Away from Ellie and those eyes that drew him in.

So he was running away? Acting like a coward now? What else was he supposed to do?

Face up to her. Get past that kiss.

Luca didn't miss a step as he spun around and headed back to the outpatients' room, right up to where Ellie was straightening up again. Reaching for her, he drew her close and lowered his head.

Just before his mouth claimed hers he muttered, 'This has got to stop. We need to move past whatever's causing us to act out of character.' Then he kissed her. Long and hard, tasting her, letting her taste him. Feeling the moment when the tension left her body and she melted in against him. Feeling those lush breasts pressed against the hard wall of his chest. Sensing her heightened awareness of him.

His growing need strained against his trousers, about to push against the softness of her belly.

Luca tore his mouth away, dropped his hands to his sides, glared into Ellie's startled eyes, and growled, 'There, we've got that out of the way. Now we can work together without any distractions.'

And he walked away. If he could call his rapid shuffle a walk.

How had he come up with all that stuff? No distractions? He'd just made a monumental error and ramped up the distraction meter to such a level it was off the Richter scale. And he'd thought he couldn't get any more stupid. Went to show how wrong a guy could be when diverted by a beautiful woman. So much for bravery. He had not intended on kissing Ellie when he returned to her.

So why had he gone back?

He seriously had no idea. Other than not wanting to be thought of as a coward. Which only went to show what an idiot he really was. Kissing Ellie again had not dampened down his ardour. Hell no. Now he wanted more. More kisses, more touching, more of everything.

Good one, Chirsky, good one.

Idiot.

Ellie's fingers were soft on her lips, tracing where Luca's mouth had touched hers. *Stunned* didn't begin to describe how she felt. When Luca had charged back into the room with a determined expression darkening his face she'd had no idea what it was about. There'd been a moment when she'd wondered if he was angry at her for some misdemeanour, except she hadn't been here long enough to stuff up anything. But then he'd hauled her into his arms and kissed her—thoroughly. Not angrily.

She'd kissed him back equally enthusiastically. It had been a kiss to defy all kisses. It shouldn't have happened. But it had, and now Ellie had to work out a way forward. In Luca's eyes that kiss should end all speculation and leave them free to get back to being who they were to each other. Friends without benefits.

'Ellie?' Louise stood before her, that worried look of two days ago back in her kind eyes. 'Are you all right?'

I've just been kissed by my best friend. How am I supposed to feel? 'I'm fine.' Uh-oh, had Louise seen her and Luca in that embrace? 'I was checking out Took.' *Before I was interrupted.* 'She's got a chest infection.' *I was checking out Luca, too, but that doesn't count. Not much. I think his chest is okay. Nah, it's hard and muscular and I want to run my tongue the length of it. Much more than okay.*

'That's Took's second infection in three weeks. I don't think there's a lot of clean water at home for keeping the wound site under her arm sterile.' Louise was studying Ellie with a very wise expression on her face. 'When you're done here, would you like me to show you how the outpatients is run instead of you working with Luca in the amputation clinic?'

Ellie knew Louise had been looking forward to a morning off to go into town. Tempting as her offer was, Ellie couldn't accept. She was here to help, not hinder the running of the clinic and the staff's downtime. 'Not at all. I've been looking forward to meeting some of those other patients.'

'As long as you're sure.'

'Louise—' Ellie grimaced '—I'm sorry. Luca and I used to be very close friends and then life got in the way. It's the best thing that could've happened, finding him working here. Truly.' On a long, slow breath she added, 'I've missed him a lot and I think he feels the same. Things have just got out of whack, but we'll settle down. You'll see. I do not want to upset anything going on here. I came to help, not disrupt.'

Finally she got a big smile from Louise. 'Any time you feel like a glass of wine and a girl talk you know where to find me.'

'You're a champ. Now I need to get some antibiotics for Took.'

'I'll walk down to the drug cupboard with you. Aaron wants some mild painkillers for his patient.'

One of the many notches in Ellie's tummy loosened. 'I heard the markets are only open in the mornings. Is that right?'

'That's what the brochures say but I've never found them closed before late afternoon yet. Aaron and I usually go there at least one afternoon a week and carry on to a bar and restaurant. Want to join us this afternoon after everyone's wrapped up here? Luca's coming,' she added quickly.

'I'd love to.' She wasn't going to let that kiss spoil her getting out and seeing the sights and enjoying shopping in the local places. Doing that with people who already knew their way around would be more fun, too. She wasn't into getting lost and trying to find her way around. Didn't have the patience, for a start. 'There's something about markets I adore.'

'You're a softie. I can see you buying from every stall.'

'Could be a long day,' she agreed. 'It will be fun.' Hopefully Luca would see things in the same light and not get het up about her joining them. Otherwise he could be the one to miss out. She wasn't going to stay back in her room. And the added bonus was more time spent with Luca. She had an itch to quieten.

'Hey, Ellie, come meet Ash,' Luca called out the moment she walked into the clinic. He was all professional and outwardly friendly. Almost as if that kiss hadn't happened. Or was on hold?

He'd got himself all together quick enough. Guess that meant he wasn't as rattled as she'd been. Still was. But then Luca had had plenty of experience at hiding what he didn't want any-one else to know about him. She tried to follow his example and focused on the boy. 'Hi, Ash. Why do we call you that?'

Luca explained, 'Because his name is longer than the alphabet and equally unpronounceable for Westerners. It starts with *A* so he's called Ash.' Luca was squatting beside a boy who couldn't be more than four, and had only one leg.

'Makes a lot of sense—not.'

When Luca looked up at her she found smiling at him wasn't too difficult. There were no recriminations peeking out, no annoyance with her for succumbing to his kiss. So she could even begin to think he might have been right—they'd needed to get that second kiss out of the way to move on. Really? Make that a no, but she'd do her best not to show how much she wanted to follow up on it.

Kneeling beside Ash, she turned to concentrate on the boy's stump. 'This happened recently? Two or three weeks ago?'

Luca nodded. 'Three. We're still getting the hang of using crutches, aren't we, Ash?'

The boy nodded slowly, his huge dark eyes sombre as he studied her, still staying close to

Luca. As if he trusted his doctor for everything. That was wonderful.

The boy was so young, younger than most she'd seen around here so far. 'Does Ash stay here all the time or is he a day patient?'

Luca locked his gaze on her and that was when she saw the apprehension in the backs of his eyes. So he wasn't being blasé about her or their kiss, just working on keeping it in perspective. But he answered the question she'd voiced, not the one spinning around her skull about where they went from that moment back in the treatment room. 'Ash is living with us for now. His mum and dad visit whenever they can get in from their village, which is up in the hills north of here.'

In other words not very often. Ellie's heart squeezed for this brave little guy, and she put her own concerns aside. 'How many brothers and sisters have you got, Ash?'

Ash stared at her for a moment, before turning to Luca for an interpretation. 'Four' was the answer.

'I can see why you've learned some of the language,' Ellie told Luca. 'These kids need you to understand them, don't they?' It had to be hideous finding themselves with such awful injuries in a clinic surrounded by people speaking strange words. Yet Luca chattered to Ash as though he was totally au fait with the boy's language. She asked, 'How do you say I like you?'

Luca nodded in understanding and slowly enunciated a phase that was almost incomprehensible.

Ellie grinned at Ash and tried to repeat the phrase. 'Don't think I'm making any sense to him at all.' She laughed.

'Try again after me.'

Same sound, same result, except Ash was starting to smile at her. A slow awakening that lifted his sad face and lightened those eyes to a dark brown, the blackness dissipating.

When Luca told him what she'd been trying to say his little smile grew and he nodded at her before putting his tiny hand on her arm.

That felt like the best thing to happen to her. After Luca's amazing kiss, that was. A quick glance at Luca and she found him watching her so intently her cheeks began heating up.

'Ash likes you, too.' His words were a caress, making her think there was more to what he said. Luca liked her, too?

Right, let's get this show on the road and stop mooning over Luca. 'Can I help him with his crutches?'

'Sure. We've just had a new pair made, which in clinic speak means an old pair cut down to Ash's size. The ones he's been using were way too big for him and he kept tripping, which caused awful pain.' Luca was all doctor mode now.

'So he's not going to be keen to get moving on these newer ones.'

'You got it.' Luca ruffled the boy's hair in that casual yet caring manner he did so well. Had he ever thought about having his own family? A warmth trickled through her at the thought of Luca surrounded by his own children.

'Is there an adult pair somewhere?' she asked and grinned when Luca's eyes widened in understanding.

'Why have I never thought of that? Over in that walk-in cupboard.' He nodded in the direction of two doors butted up together. 'Have you ever had to use crutches yourself?'

'Nope. But that's the point. I can make mistakes, too.'

'This I have to watch.' Luca chuckled as she headed for the cupboard.

Trying the crutches out for size, she quickly had a pair and started back to Ash, swinging between the wooden implements that had seen better days a long time ago. It wasn't as easy as she'd thought it would be, but that was fine. She didn't want to be perfect in front of the boy. She'd rather fall over and laugh. Though she didn't want Ash falling. For him it would be too painful. 'Let's go.' She nodded at him.

Ash stared at her, not making any move to get off the chair. Two big tears slid down his cheeks and he shook his head from side to side.

Ah, hell. Tears would be her undoing any time. She'd rather wrap him up in a blanket and read him a story than make him do this. But, 'Come on. You'll be good.'

Luca held out the small crutches and said something in Laotian. Whatever it was his voice was soothing and encouraging, and slowly Ash stood up on his good leg and took the crutches being held out to him.

Go you, Luca. 'We'll do this together,' Ellie said and, standing on one foot, moved her crutches forward and waited.

Luca interpreted.

Ash bit into his bottom lip and his face crunched up in concentration.

Ellie held her breath.

So did Luca.

Ash lifted the crutches and put them farther in front of him.

'Go you. Now we hop.' Ellie demonstrated, making sure she didn't go too far forward.

Luca interpreted.

Ash hopped. The crutches wobbled dangerously.

Ellie held her breath as Luca held his hands beneath Ash's arms without actually touching him, ready to catch him if the crutches went from under him.

Panic flared in Ash's eyes as he swayed and grappled for balance. When he was standing straight again he looked down at the crutches as though they were to blame for his predicament.

'That's good, Ash.' Ellie kept her tone light and encouraging. 'Now we'll do it again.' And again, and again.

Slowly they progressed across the room, and with every step Ash's confidence grew. The fear softened from his face as determination crept into his eyes, tightened his mouth. He was going to make these crutches work no matter what.

'Don't get too cocky,' Ellie warned. A fall onto the floor would set him back again.

'Take a break,' Luca told her, and then repeated the same thing to Ash in Laotian.

Or she supposed that was what he was saying. 'I'll stop if Ash does.'

Ash said nothing, just turned and began crossing the room back to where they'd started.

Ellie hurried to catch up, nearly tripping over her own feet. Ash looked at her and almost laughed. Almost but not quite. His mouth widened, his eyes lit up and his chest lifted, then everything stopped and he went back to solemn. Guess he didn't do laughing since the devastation that had brought him to the clinic's attention. Life for these kids would become very hard when they grew up and had to struggle to compete for work in an environment not flush with jobs and cash even for the uninjured.

She wasn't going to let that distract them from having fun while he learned to get around. This was only the first step of learning to be mobile again. 'You little ratbag.' She grinned. 'It's a game now, is it?' She held back on racing him. He was not ready for that yet. But it wouldn't be long before he was running around on those sticks as though born with them. Ellie reckoned that soon the staff would be wishing he'd sit down and keep still for a while. 'I am so glad I came here.'

Luca grinned. 'Glad you see it that way. I get such a kick from helping these guys.'

'You're a natural with children.'

He looked shocked. 'I am?'

'Definitely.' And what was more, she really liked that. How come she'd never noticed it before?

'Luca,' Sharon, a nurse, called across the room. 'There's been an accident outside the clinic and the victim's been brought in here. His heart's stopped so there's no time to wait for an ambulance to take him next door.'

Luca said, 'Coming. Get Carol to take over with Ash. Ellie, can you join me?'

'Be right there.' She helped Ash put down his crutches and sit on his seat again. His legs were shaking from the strain of learning to balance and hop, but his eyes were wide with excitement.

'I'm here.' Carol sank down on the chair beside the boy. 'We'll do some exercises and rubbing on your muscles now, Ash.' Carol was a physiotherapist and had a love-hate relationship with the children for the pain and relief she brought them.

Ellie dashed to the small resus unit, where an elderly man lay on the bed. Luca was already leaning over him performing CPR while a nurse gave oxygen as required.

'There's a defib in Theatre,' Luca told her.

Ellie raced to get it and, returning, opened the kit and began attaching the pads. 'Stand back, everyone.' After checking everyone was out of the way she pressed the start button and held her breath as the mechanical voice recited the procedure that was underway. The patient's body arched off the bed, dropped back. Instantly the cardiac monitor began beeping instead of the flat tone it had been giving.

'Hoorah.' A muted cheer went up.

Luca stepped back and wiped the sweat from his brow with the back of his hand. 'Strike one to us. Might as well sort out those wounds while he's here. I wonder which came first—the accident or the cardiac arrest?' he said as he began examining the man thoroughly.

Ellie shook her head in amazement as she tossed her gloves into a bin half an hour later and watched their patient being wheeled through the building to the hospital annex. 'That's one lucky man. Who gets catapulted through the front windscreen, lands on a pole in a ditch and only gets concussion with lacerations and bruising?'

'You're forgetting the heart attack that probably caused him to drive off the road in the first place.' Luca rubbed his eyes with his fingertips.

'He chose the right spot for his accident,' Ellie said as she watched Luca. There were shadows under his eyes. 'Are you having trouble sleeping?' she asked before she engaged her brain in gear. What if he said he'd lain awake last night thinking about that first kiss? She wouldn't know how to handle that. It was bad enough having to work with him and pretend they hadn't kissed a second time, and that the entire staff probably knew about it because little children knew no boundaries when it came to being discreet.

'It was hotter than usual last night,' Luca muttered without looking at her.

'Really?' A little devil was making her question things best left alone. The same devil that had her wanting more of Luca's kisses. 'I didn't notice.'

'You've only been here a few days. All the night temperatures will be hot to you.' Luca's gloves headed in the same direction as hers. 'Coffee?' he asked, then looked shocked for asking.

The devil replied, 'Sure. Why not? Unless we're needed in the clinic again.' She should be wishing they were. But she wasn't.

'We're due a break.'

Ellie followed Luca to the kitchen. 'What's next on the list of things to do?'

As Luca stirred a load of sugar into his coffee he said, 'This afternoon I'm visiting two villages where we have kids still adjusting to their prostheses. You're coming with me.'

'Great. Seeing where these families live will be interesting.'

'It's a damned eye-opener is what it is. Don't go expecting a pretty picture, Ellie, otherwise you'll get a rude shock.' His voice was laced with anger. At her?

Taken aback, she snapped, 'I said interesting, not exciting or fun.'

'Good. Then, we'll head out after lunch.'

'I'll let Louise know. She's expecting us to join her for the market and a meal afterwards.'

'No need. She knows where we're going, and that we'll catch up with her and Aaron at the market.' His tone hadn't lightened.

'What's your problem? If you'd prefer I didn't come with you then just say so. I won't be offended.' *I might be hurt a wee bit, but I'll get over it.* If he didn't want to be shut in a vehicle with her for the afternoon then he didn't, but he could at least tell her. Didn't need to go all grumpy on her.

'You need to see these people in their own villages. It will help you understand better how much they have to give up when they visit their children, why they often send another child to be with the injured one.'

'Will it help me to accept that these kids have to dig for metal in order to have food at the end of the day?' she growled back. Two could get wound up and snap at each other.

Luca's shoulders lifted as he drew a deep breath. 'Unfortunately yes, but it won't help you condone it. Nothing, no one, would. Those bombs are so destructive. But hunger is worse— or so the villagers think. As they're the ones living with it, who am I to argue?'

Instantly her mood softened. Whatever was going on between her and Luca, her job was about these children and their families, and her time here was about her job. Somehow she'd get through the time spent in close proximity to Luca without going off her head yearning for another kiss. Fingers crossed.

CHAPTER SIX

'WE'RE GOING TO see Lai first.' Luca drove slowly around a group of schoolchildren on bikes. 'She's a fourteen-year-old who had the misfortune to fall into a crater and land on large pieces of shrapnel, piercing her abdomen and perforating her bowel.'

'Unbelievable.' Ellie grimaced. 'Did Lai work or go to school before this happened?'

'She worked the family stall at a nearby market selling vegetables that the village grew. Now someone else does that job and she tries to look after some of the gardens, but she's weak and suffers a lot of pain and inflammation that we haven't been able to control very successfully.' Luca had a box in the back of the vehicle for vegetables he'd buy from Lai to take back to their kitchen. Any little amount helped the village a lot.

'They're a tough people, aren't they?'

He nodded. 'They are. Here we go.' He pulled into a yard where hens were fossicking for any unfortunate worm or beetle. 'That's Lai over in the shade.' The girl looked as though she were dozing but sat upright the moment he stepped out of the four-wheel drive. 'Hi, Lai.'

'Dr Luca. I didn't know you were coming today. Who's that?' She nodded at Ellie.

'This is Dr Thompson. She works at the clinic with me.' He kept the words simple because he didn't understand the language as well as Ellie had given him credit for.

But Lai must've understood. 'Has she come to see me?'

'Yes.'

'She's pretty.'

At least that was what Luca thought Lai said. And if it was he had to agree. Ellie was pretty, downright beautiful really, with her high cheek-bones and sparkling hazel eyes that sometimes were more green than brown—like today. Then there was all that dark blonde hair she'd tied in a high ponytail to keep it off her neck. As it swung with her movements it made him itch to let the hair free and run his hands over and through it, to feel if it was as silken as it looked. 'Lai says you're pretty,' he told El. He'd always known that but never got in a stew over her looks. Now they did things to his libido that shouldn't be happening.

'What does she want from me?' Ellie smiled towards the girl. 'Hello, Lai. My name is Ellie.'

Luca translated roughly, and earned Ellie the biggest smile he'd ever seen the girl give anyone. El did that everywhere she went. All the children at the clinic adored her already, their little faces lighting up the moment she stepped into their room. She was so good with them. Like today with Ash and those crutches no one had been able to get him back to using since his last tumble. Now the kid was almost racing on them.

Already Ellie was squatting down, holding Lai's hand and talking softly. It didn't seem to matter that Lai didn't understand her words; she certainly understood that compassion and care radiating from Ellie's face.

'You're like old friends,' he mock growled. 'Yakety-yak.'

Ellie squinted up at him. 'You can join in. It's what friends do.'

Was that a poke at him? Because of that kiss? 'I'll get the medical bag.' Anything to give him a break from those eyes that saw too damned much. He shouldn't have brought her out here today. It had been the perfect opportunity to get away alone for a couple of hours while he re-lived that kiss and put it to bed in his mind. Put it to bed? He knew exactly what he wanted to put to bed and with whom. Making love to Ellie shouldn't even enter his mind, but it had from around the instant he'd started kissing her the other evening. And it sure as hell didn't seem in any hurry to go away again.

His knuckles were white where he clenched the bag's carry strap. How was he supposed to get through the coming weeks if this was how he felt after only days? Look at her. Chatting with Lai as if she knew the language and mak-ing the girl laugh. Now there was a first. Lai didn't laugh, ever.

But hey, he understood perfectly. Ellie made him smile more often than he had lately, so bogged down in what to do next with his career that he'd become unable to find his usual cheery persona. She made him feel other things, too, like excitement for being with her, for being alive. Like this need to hold her and make love with her. His friend, best friend back in the days they lived and worked together. Never had he felt a twinge of desire for her, and yet now his whole body pulsed with a throbbing need that would not go away. Damn it.

He slammed the door shut, the bang echoing through the village. Ellie raised questioning eyes in his direction and stood up. 'You okay?'

'Why wouldn't I be?' Hell, he was turning into an old grump. A smiling old grump. 'I need to take Lai's temperature and check her wounds.'

'Want me to do it?'

No, I want you to take a hike, give me some space and stop looking so damned desirable in that thin-strapped top that barely reaches your waist and those short shorts. 'Come with us into Lai's family home.' He should've insisted she dress in a shirt with sleeves down to her wrists and baggy trousers that didn't outline her butt so well.

The tiny lopsided dwelling was spotless, an amazing feat considering the dust swirling around outside. Lai's mother was cooking rice and something he couldn't make out by smell or sight. She gave him a shy smile and shifted a stool out from under the table for him.

'Your temperature is normal today,' he told Lai. That was a first. Hopefully that indicated the start of Lai's return to full health.

'The wound looks clear of infection, too,' Ellie said a moment later.

Luca asked to see Lai's pills and gave her some more antibiotics to take if redness returned at the wound site. Then he negotiated to buy some vegetables from her mother and soon he and Ellie were back on the road.

A few minutes along the road and Ellie started laughing.

'What?' he asked. 'Have you got heatstroke?'

She only laughed louder. 'I'm trying to put

Luca the A and E specialist and Luca the Laos clinic doctor together. It's not easy.'

'Thanks a bunch. I don't think I'm a bad doctor. I do an all right job anywhere I'm needed.' Didn't he?

Her hand suddenly covered his on the steering wheel. 'Relax. I wasn't having a poke at you. You're an amazing doctor.'

A different heat from that of the climate seeped into his blood, warmed him deep inside. 'Thanks.' For the compliment? Or the touch? He hoped she forgot her hand was there for a little while.

'I'm still getting used to seeing you working here where the urgency is less—except when new patients turn up bleeding all over the show. I only remember you on full alert, going from patient to patient, giving each of them your undivided attention, and yelling orders to the nurses. Here you're calmer, work at a pace that suits the children and still get to see twice as many patients as everyone else.'

Quite a speech. His chest swelled with pride. 'Coming here has been good for me. But I want to return to emergency medicine some time in the near future.' When had he made that decision? Only a couple of days ago he'd been wondering whether to take up a twelve-month contract in Cambodia. Was Ellie's presence changing everything for him? 'Would you give up what you do back home and spend a year doing something similar?'

She withdrew her hand.

Damn.

Ellie nibbled her bottom lip for a moment. 'I don't think so. But it's early days. Ask me again at the end of my month here.'

One month. It could be a very long time, or it could speed by. With Ellie he had times when the minutes seemed to whizz past, and then when he was busting to kiss her again and had to work with her instead the minutes felt like hours. Now he had to sit in a car with her so close his skin was constantly aware of her. He should've hosed her off before they left to remove that tantalising scent she wore.

She hadn't finished telling him about what she was doing next. 'I've already got a six-month contract back home starting after Christmas. Any ideas of working offshore will have to wait.'

'Christmas. Being here I'd sort of forgotten about it. You'll be spending the day with your family?'

'I don't think so.' There was a sharp edge in her voice.

'Why not?' She had always tried to get home if she wasn't rostered to work on the twenty-fifth.

'I'll be in Auckland.' A definite 'don't ask' echoed between them.

But this was his friend; he needed to know. 'There are planes.'

'I don't want to be in the same city as Freddy, all right?'

Didn't make sense to him. It wasn't as though Freddy would be sitting down to Christmas dinner with her parents. 'We used to talk about things that were bugging us.'

'We did.' She stared straight ahead.

Okay. He'd fall into line and stop pushing her. He didn't want her wrath, nor did he want to upset her, and it seemed that was where he might be headed, though for the life of him he didn't understand why. 'You're going to love the market. Hope you've brought lots of cash.'

'They don't use EFTPOS?' She looked relieved that he'd changed the subject.

What had that been about? He hoped she'd tell him sometime before she headed back home.

'Buy this one.' Luca passed her a hat from a stall table to try on. 'The kids will fall over laughing if you wear that around the place.'

Ellie took the cotton creation with fabric elephants and bears swinging from the brim. 'The kids or you?' She chuckled. She put down the sane and sensible sunhat she'd just tried and plopped Luca's suggestion on her head.

The woman behind the counter grinned and pointed to a mirror. 'You like? You buy?' The hope in her voice would've had Ellie buying the hat if nothing else would.

'Go on, and this one.' She handed over the sensible one, and picked up two more brightly coloured caps. 'And these.'

'You've only got one head,' Luca quipped.

'They're not exactly expensive,' she retorted, happily handing over some American dollars.

'You're supposed to barter.' Luca shook his head at her. That smile that had started as he followed her around Talaat Sao, the morning market that ran all day, just got bigger and bigger. So he was enjoying her company. On the trip to the villages she'd begun to believe he couldn't wait for her to be gone.

'Next time.' Not. She hated bartering. Wasn't any good at it because she felt it was cheating someone out of their money.

Luca only laughed. 'I'll do it for you.'

Aaron called from farther along. 'Luca, here are some shirts that might be what you're looking for.'

While Luca headed that way Ellie waited for her change and the hats to be folded neatly and placed in a plastic bag. *'Kowp jai,'* she said, and smiled at the woman's surprise at her butchered thank-you.

The woman nodded and grinned. *'Kowp jai.'*

That sounded nothing like what Ellie had said, but, hey, she'd tried. Turning in the direction

Luca had gone, she scanned the heads of the crowd pushing through the narrow walkways between overladen stalls and couldn't see him or Aaron. Luca's height had him shoulders above most people and he was nowhere to be seen. Making her way to where she thought Aaron had called from, she found dozens of shirts hanging for sale but no sight of the two men. Or Louise. Where were they? How would she find them? If she went outside she could end up on the wrong side and not know where to go next.

She stared around, ignoring the bumps from people trying to move through the crowd. *Think, Ellie. Getting freaked out is stupid. It's not a massive market. They won't have gone far.* Looking at the next stall, she saw there were more shirts for sale, as there were at all the stalls along this line. She began walking quickly, suddenly wanting nothing more than to see Luca.

If she didn't find them along here she'd return to the stall where she'd got her hats and wait for them to find her.

'Ellie, come and tell Luca he should buy that shirt,' Louise called from behind her.

Spinning around, she saw the three people she'd been searching for crammed into a back corner of a stall she'd walked straight past. 'You think he'll listen to me?' She gave a lopsided smile and hoped her racing heart settled fast. How silly to get all worked up over not being able to see these guys for all of five minutes.

'Depends what you've got to say.' Luca looked at her across the tiny space. 'Hey.' He shrugged out of the shirt. 'I'll take it.' Then he crossed to her and gripped her hands, bag of hats included. 'Breathe deep. You're okay. You're not in that underground cave now.' His fingers tightened around her hands, his thumbs rubbing her wrists. 'You're fine. Promise.'

See? Her friend understood her, knew why she'd got worked up over nothing. 'I looked around and couldn't find you. I didn't know where to go, where we'd come in.'

'Ellie? You okay?' Louise looked at her with concern.

She let go a sigh. 'Yes, sorry. Years back a group of us went to some caves and when we were all deep inside the guides turned the lights off for a short time so we could see the glow worms. I got a bit lost and panicked. Ever since I get a wee bit stressed in crowds if I'm not sure where I am.'

Luca kissed her fingers before dropping her hands. 'My fault. Knowing how you were that day, I shouldn't have left you at that stall on your own.'

'No, Luca, it's not your fault. I'm a big girl. I should've watched where you went and kept an eye on you until I had my shopping sorted.' She liked that he had recognised her panic instantly and had come to her. That was special, and she felt cared for.

'Should we head out for that drink, then?' Aaron asked.

'No way. I haven't seen half the market yet. And I know Louise is looking for some earrings to send home to her niece.' She wasn't preventing everyone doing what they'd come here for. Anyway, her panic had gone, she was with Luca and all was well in her world.

'Trinkets and jewellery next, then.' Louise nodded her approval.

By the time they all sat down to beer and wine at a local bar Ellie was pleased with her shopping. 'Those earrings are lovely.' She sipped her drink.

'Which ones?' Luca drawled. 'I thought the stall holder was going to faint with excitement the number you two bought.'

'Says the guy who bought five shirts,' Louise said.

'I can't wait to visit the craft galleries,' Ellie enthused. 'Handwoven fabrics and embroidery will get me every time.' And might put a bit of a dent in her bank account, especially if her baggage allowance was exceeded going home. But, hey, what was money for if not sharing around? She knew she was a sucker for the shy smiles on the faces of the women selling their wares.

'He knows you well.' Louise nodded at Luca when he leaned on the bar waiting for the barman's attention so he could order a snack.

'He does.' Better than anyone else, Ellie realised with a start. Not even her ex had known her as well. Whose fault had that been? Hers for not offering up titbits about herself, or Freddy's for not thinking to ask? 'It's kind of good having someone aware of who I am.' It was something she hadn't had for a while.

'And it helps that that someone has a nice butt,' Louise said, grinning in the direction of Luca.

Aaron's eyes rolled.

'What are you trying to do here?' Ellie asked, while trying not to gape at what was truly a very nice butt. She was a butt girl after all.

Louise shrugged through a soft smile. 'Nothing.'

Now *her* eyes were rolling. 'Of course.' Where had this longing for something more with Luca come from? Kisses were great, but what would making love with him be like? Shock rippled through her, bringing a sweat to her arms, between her breasts, her thighs. Sex with Luca? Yeah, that too-good-looking-to-be-true man. Was it even possible to go from best friends to lovers? Her skin heated further at the thought.

I really do *want to find out, want to match my body to his and feel him inside me.*

The glass shook in her hand, but she dared not set it down for fear of knocking it over.

Sex with Luca and there'd be problems. Keep

him as a friend, and they'd always get along no matter how many arguments they had over the dumbest of things. In her experience friends were more forgiving than husbands. Take Luca as a lover and everything expanded, became filled with tension and the potential for hurt feelings that no one recovered from. She trusted Luca as a friend. It might not be the same if he became her lover. There was more to lose.

A dose of reality was needed about now to stop her head spinning. She checked her phone in a pathetic hope that she was needed back at the clinic. Nothing doing. She reached for her glass and forced her mind to follow the conversation Luca and Aaron were now having about deep-sea fishing in the South Pacific. She hadn't known Luca had tried it. Hadn't known he enjoyed fishing, even.

Next they headed to a restaurant filled with loud tourists, and followed that up with a nightcap at a nightclub so that she could apparently see more of the city.

'Can't have you going home without seeing every side of Vientiane.' Aaron grinned. 'Hope you're into dancing.'

'There's no music.' She stated the obvious, staring at Luca and fighting the sense she was slipping into a deep hole with no way out. She couldn't dance with Luca. That would mean touching him, feeling those muscles moving under her hand.

Luca chimed in. 'There will be. Very loud, too. The band's taking a break.' He leaned close and asked, 'What do you want to drink?'

As she breathed in his scent her mouth dried while her skin heated. 'W-water,' she managed, wanting to grab him to prevent him moving away. She turned her head, her nose brushing across his cheek. 'Luca?' she whispered.

'Ye-es?' He remained perfectly still.

What? Luca what? Her mind was blank, totally absorbed in all things Luca and unable to come up with a single word.

Finally he stepped away. 'Two waters,' he said to the barman before pulling a stool close to hers and parking that very nice butt down.

Her lungs struggled with the whole in-out thing. Air seemed lodged somewhere between her nose and her chest. Was she ill? Could that be what this was all about?

You're kidding. You've got the hots for Luca. That's what it's about, nothing more, nothing less.

Right. Now what? She stared around the club, finally focusing on Louise and Aaron on the dance floor. 'They're a lovely couple.'

Luca's gaze followed hers. 'I wonder sometimes if they don't get enough privacy. Living on the compound all the time means there are always others around.'

'I wouldn't cope with that. I like my own space, and if I was with someone I'd want him to myself some of the day.' Yet she and Freddy hadn't spent hours together at home. One or other of them was usually working long hours or he'd be playing golf or she'd be at the movies. It hadn't bothered her then. Over the past couple of days her marriage had started to look a little different from what she'd believed it to be. Had she been an unknowing part of its breakdown? There were usually two sides to everything.

As that blinding truth struck her, Luca took the glass from her hand. 'Let's dance.' Before she could say no he was leading her onto the floor to join other couples dancing to the fast tempo. Luca held on to her hand and began to move in time to the music.

Ellie found a smile for him. 'You always were a smooth dude on the dance floor.'

His face cracked into a wide smile. 'You bet.' And he grabbed her to spin them around in a wide circle, scattering half the other people nearby. 'Glad you remembered.'

There wasn't a lot she'd forgotten, just things she hadn't known about until this week. What else hadn't he spoken about? She wanted to know it all, felt the need to understand more about him. Why was he here and not in that A and E department? That had nothing to do with Gaylene's betrayal, surely? Why didn't he know what he wanted to do next in his life? That might be because he'd lost his child. Something that big would change her focus, too.

The music changed, much slower this time, and Ellie found herself being tucked against Luca's body, one of his hands around her waist, the other holding hers against his chest, as they stepped in unison to the rhythm. Their hips touched, her breasts moved over his chest as she danced, and she breathed him in. She forgot all the questions she'd wanted to ask. Forgot all the reasons why she shouldn't be dancing like this with Luca. Knew only his heat, his scent, his hard body against hers.

She didn't want to go back to her tiny, stuffy room. Could stay here in Luca's arms all night. Being held so tenderly almost broke her heart. She hadn't known such tenderness before. Yet there was strength in his hands and body, in his face too. His beloved face. How had she forgotten the warmth in his eyes? In his heart, his hands?

She'd never really noticed it. That was how. Luca had been a friend. Now he was more than that. And somehow she had to ignore the desire unfurling deep inside her body, not let it take over and rule her besotted brain. But she'd wait for one more song before she shifted out of his hold. Just one more.

No one told the band that she didn't want to step away from Luca and minutes later they were dancing all over the show at a fast pace.

Ellie's mood lifted as she jived and shook in

time to some of her all-time favourite songs, Luca moving right along with her.

'Time we headed home,' Aaron interrupted. 'Unless you want to grab a cab later.'

Luca raised an eyebrow at Ellie.

Yes, she'd love nothing more than to continue dancing the night away, but she really had to remember she and Luca were no more than friends. That to take this any further might help her heart for a while but it would only get broken all over again when Luca had had enough. Or finally made up his mind where he was going next because that wouldn't be in the same direction as she was headed. Unfortunately. Because she was beginning to see a future that involved Luca, despite knowing it was impossible. 'We're coming with you.'

'We are?' Luca stretched that eyebrow higher.

'I am.' She shrugged. 'Sorry, but— Well, I'm sorry.'

He draped an arm over her shoulders. 'Not a problem, El. Glad one of us is thinking straight.'

Couldn't he look a little bit disappointed?

CHAPTER SEVEN

A WEEK AFTER that night dancing at the club Ellie was still vacillating between relief she'd insisted she came back from the nightclub with the others and wishing she'd given into the relentless need to learn more about Luca and that incredible body.

'Ellie, come and play.' A young boy stood in front of her, swinging a cricket bat from side to side.

How incongruous was that? Cricket in Laos seemed unlikely yet someone previously working here had introduced the game to the kids and apparently they couldn't get enough of it. Given the falls and knocks the kids received, the staff had to limit the number of games. She put her laptop aside and stood up, stretching her calves when they protested at the sudden change in position. 'Sure. Who else is playing?'

'Everyone,' she was told. 'They're waiting over the road.'

Over on the vacant land where houses used to stand before they burned to the ground in a dreadful misadventure years ago. 'Right, have you got the ball and the wickets?'

'Yes, Ellie, we have.' This little guy enjoyed practising his English. He wanted to be a truck driver one day and take tourists everywhere. 'Dr Luca got them.'

Of course Luca would be playing. If the kids were involved, then so was Luca. They could have a team each. This was the first time she'd joined in, but she'd seen a game the other day and had admired the kids for their determination and strength. Some swung crutches, another waved an arm that had been cut off at the elbow. All of them carried scars on some part of their body. All of them were laughing and chatting like monkeys in a tree. She loved the lot of them.

Noi called out from the clinic front door, 'You want a wicket keeper?' He'd never admit it but she'd heard he loved cricket as much as the youngsters. He also kept the children in line, gently admonishing them when they got carried away with heaving the ball at the wicket and their pal holding the bat. Even tennis balls could hurt when hitting the wrong spot on a small body.

'You bet,' Luca yelled back.

'I'm first batting,' said the boy who'd asked her to join them.

'I'm throwing the ball,' said another.

'Shouldn't we have teams?' she asked no one in particular.

'I want to be in Dr Luca's,' someone yelled.

'Me, too.'

A girl said shyly, 'I'm playing with Ellie.'

'You know what? I've got a plan. Noi, can you bring some crutches out here? Our size.' She tugged the belt off her shorts and handed it to Luca. 'Strap my leg up so I'm the same as these guys.'

Luca's eyes widened. 'You're kidding, right? That's going to be very uncomfortable.'

'Like it is for the kids all the time,' Ellie parried. 'You can tie one arm to your chest so that you can't use it.'

'You're nuts,' but Luca took her belt and tied up her leg.

She tried not to notice when his fingers touched her skin. Tried really hard. Then he pulled his shirt off and somehow managed to make one arm useless by twisting the shirt around his neck and tying it over his arm. She had to focus on the ground so as to avoid staring at the view created when he'd removed that shirt.

'Completely bonkers,' he told her with the first spontaneous smile she'd received from him all week.

What was bonkers? Oh. Her idea that all the staff out here were now partaking in by incapacitating themselves in some way. Not her longing for Luca. So much for putting the brakes on her highly fired-up hormones the other night. She'd been uptight ever since, and he'd been reacting the same way whenever he was around her. It might've been for the best if they had made love and got it out of the way.

'Bet no one back home has seen a cricket game

quite like this.' Ellie laughed half an hour later as she lay sprawled on the ground after tripping over her crutch for the third time. 'Running for the ball and making catches is incredibly difficult but a whole heap of fun.'

'It was a great idea.' Luca nodded as he tried to get his breathing under control after chasing a ball right across the field. 'The kids are loving this more than ever.'

'So are you.' He looked the most relaxed she'd seen him for days.

He nodded. 'You know what I like best about working here?' He didn't wait for her to answer. 'We're not only doctors but physiotherapists, psychologists and friends to these kids. It's the whole package.'

'Changing your thinking about returning to emergency medicine?' It would be a shame. He was so good at it, but then again he was proving to be good at this. He was starting to become involved with people in a way he'd never done before. It suddenly struck Ellie with blinding clarity why Luca had chosen emergency medicine over all other specialties—he could treat people and send them home or to a specialist, but he didn't have to know who they were outside the emergency department. No learning about their family or their job, or whether they liked sports or were couch potatoes. He worked in the immediate picture with no tomorrows.

Ellie sat up and looked at this man she'd thought she knew. Back then she hadn't even started getting behind his facade. He'd fooled her as much as everyone else. Kind of undermined their friendship. When she'd thought they shared most things about themselves Luca had been holding back big time. She should be annoyed, angry even, but no. She was liking him more and more each day. This revelation only made her more determined to get to know Luca better, properly, and not only in the physical way. In fact that could take a hike for a while so that they could spend time together talking and enjoying getting out and about in Vientiane. *As if your hormones are going to settle down while you do that.* No harm in trying.

'You're staring.'

'Yes, I am.' *And liking what I see.*

A loud cry cut off whatever Luca had been about to say. A girl had tripped over her crutch and landed flat on her face. Ellie scrambled upright and raced across on her one leg and the crutch to drop down beside her. 'Lulu, let me see.' She gently removed the girl's hands from her face.

Blood spurted from Lulu's nose, and tears streamed down her cheeks. 'Hurts, Ellie.'

'I know.' Kissing Lulu's cheek, she gently felt the nose, then the rest of her face.

Luca knelt down opposite Ellie. 'What's the damage?'

'Everything seems fine,' Ellie told him, then said to Lulu, 'You've flattened your nose a bit, but it's going to be all right.'

'I don't want to play anymore.'

'Fair enough. Can I look at your back?' Lulu had three wounds zigzagging from her right shoulder to her left hip, caused by an explosion outside her school that had thrown her sky-high then dumped her on top of a wooden fence.

When Lulu nodded, Ellie carefully lifted her shirt. Phew. The stitches had held. Not that Ellie really expected otherwise, but she liked to be sure. 'I'll take you back over the road and get you a drink.'

Luca told her, 'I'll carry on with the cricket a bit longer.'

'See you later.' She began undoing the belt that held her leg bent, grimacing as pins and needles stabbed her muscles when the blood began circulating again.

'Want to go into town for a meal tonight?' He seemed to be holding his breath as he waited for her reply.

'Love to.' They could start on that talking stuff and getting to know each other better. Did that mean she'd tell him what Freddy and Caitlin had done to her? No. She wasn't going there, wasn't ready. She'd become quite adept at ignoring the truth and pretending she didn't have a sister or ex-husband—except in the middle of the night or when she was tired and not controlling her thought processes as well as she might. She wasn't any better than Luca at putting it all out there.

Lulu was crying steadily now.

'Hey, come on, poppet. Let's get you cleaned up.' She took the girl's hand and headed for the building.

Luca watched Ellie and Lulu all the way to the clinic and in through the doors that seemed to gobble them up. Ellie was a marvel, strapping her leg to be like the kids. She'd run—if using one leg and a crutch could be called running—back and forth after the ball whenever it was hit in her direction. No wonder the kids adored her. She was so natural with them. Aaron had hinted at trying to get her to take a twelve-month posting but she hadn't been very receptive.

Slap. The tennis ball bounced off his thigh. Luca looked around to find the culprit and met a pair of laughing eyes. 'Ng, you little tiger.' Reaching for the ball, he threw it at the wickets and missed by a mile, which only made the kids laugh and chase after it.

'You were daydreaming,' Ng said as he ran to the other end of the wicket. 'I got a run,' he shouted at his friends.

If the kids were noticing how distracted he'd

become he needed to do something about it. Like what?

Take Ellie to bed.

Or have a long, cold shower every thirty minutes.

Or— He had no idea. Ellie had climbed into his skull and wasn't about to be evicted. And, he huffed, he'd damned well gone and suggested they go into town tonight. Again. They'd been doing quite a bit of eating out but usually one or two of the other staff members went with them. So there was his answer. Ask around to see who else wanted to join them.

'Catch it, Luca,' someone screamed at him.

Hell. He was meant to be playing cricket. He scanned the air between him and the wicket, saw a black shadow dropping towards the ground only a couple of metres away. Lunging at it, his fingers found the ball, curved it into the palm of his hand. When he held it up for everyone to see there were shouts of jubilation and a grizzle from Ng.

'I'm on your team.'

So why am I fielding? Luca wanted to ask. But

basically if a person wasn't batting or bowling they were trying to catch the ball. No one really won, but then they didn't lose, either. 'Want to bowl next?' he asked, knowing Ng would never turn down that opportunity.

Glancing at his watch, Luca sighed. Still hours to go before he and Ellie headed into town. Hours when he'd be busy rubbing sore muscles on some of these kids caused by falls and skids in the field. It never failed to amaze him how eager they were to get into the fray, knowing they might hurt themselves. Tough little blighters, each and every one of them.

When he returned home he'd miss them all, even those he hadn't yet met. Returned home? Okay, he meant when he left Laos. Didn't he? Going back to NZ was on the cards but much further down the track. Emergency medicine still held its thrall and when he returned to that he wanted to be at the top of his game, but right now he was getting so much pleasure out of knowing his patients better than a BP reading and a diagnosis. Who'd have believed it? Not him—Mr Avoid-All-Relationships-That-Involve-

Exposing-His-Weaknesses. He liked having the kids hanging around demanding his attention. Who'd have thought it? Not him.

'Your turn.' One of the older girls stood in front of him, holding out the bat. 'But you can't hit the ball too hard.'

He grinned. 'Want to bet?'

Later, when everyone traipsed into the kitchen for food and water Ellie was there with Lulu, who looked decidedly happier now. Again Ellie had worked her magic.

She was so good with children. Where had she learned that? Or was it inherent? She'd be a brilliant mother, seemed to have all the right instincts.

As kids shouted and teased and bumped around him he heard Ellie's laughter. Raising his eyes, he met her amused gaze.

'Look at you.' She grinned. 'Not much more than a kid yourself, the way you've got chocolate icing on your chin.'

Luca ran his tongue around his lips and tried to find the icing dollop she'd mentioned. His tongue wasn't long enough. But when he looked back at Ellie she was obviously fascinated with it. Snapping his mouth shut, he turned away, trying to deny the heat zipping through his veins.

'Who's first for a massage?' he asked above the din.

Everyone got even busier eating and talking. Not one kid looked in his direction.

'Lulu's had hers,' Ellie told the kids. 'Pogo, bring that cake and come with me.'

Pogo, named for the way she usually bounced everywhere, reluctantly picked up another piece of cake and limped out of the door behind Ellie.

'Ng,' Luca said. 'Come on. The sooner we do this, the sooner you can do something more fun.'

'Can we sing?' Ng asked hopefully.

Another thing Ellie had started. Singing while massages were going on.

'Great idea. Come on, everyone. Bring that cake and follow us. We'll do this together.'

Soon the clinic was filled with the less than tuneful sounds of simple English songs Ellie had taught the children being yelled and sung and whispered. Even the other staff members helping were adding their voices. Ellie's voice was there, in tune and strong, the words clear and her face alive with joy. At that moment he'd swear she was the happiest he'd seen her since she'd arrived. Such simple pleasure had a lot going for it, and Ellie was soaking it up. He'd forgotten how much she enjoyed singing, and how she'd been an avid karaoke fan.

'The amputee clinic works a kind of magic on you, doesn't it?' Luca said as they wandered through the city centre later that night.

'It's the children who do that. They're so up-beat at times I want to bottle whatever it is that makes them that way and take it home. They're amazing.' Ellie stooped to stare into a shop window. 'Look at that. The weaving is beautiful. I'm going to have to get a piece before I go home.'

'What would you do with it?'

She lifted her shoulders, dropped them. 'No idea. It doesn't matter. A piece of handwoven fabric will make a wonderful memory of Vientiane.'

He had stored some of those lately. All with

Ellie in them, all able to go with him wherever he went. 'Along with the zillion photos you've taken.'

She never seemed to go anywhere without her camera or phone. There were probably as many pictures of the children on her phone as in her camera. 'It's going to take me months to sort through those, and pick the best for an album.'

'Do people still do that?' He was happy leaving the few he occasionally remembered to take on a stick, which meant one day he'd probably lose them. But then photography wasn't one of his passions.

'I guess it's too easy not to get photos printed these days, but I like flicking through the pages of an album. Turning on my laptop and clicking on different folders doesn't give me the same satisfaction.' Ellie continued walking along the street. 'Got loads of you, too. Wait till I show Renee the cricket-doctor shots. She won't believe it's you.'

'Renee? You two are still in touch?' She'd been one of their housemates way back.

'I've been renting a room in her apartment

since I found myself single again. She's just as bossy as she used to be.'

'And you still take no notice, I bet.'

'Something like that.' Ellie looked around. 'Where shall we eat tonight?'

'How about the restaurant tucked behind that hedge?' It was more upmarket then anywhere they'd eaten before.

Ellie's eyes widened and she turned them on him. 'Are we treating ourselves?'

'No. I'm treating you.' Out of the blue had come the need to take her somewhere better than a rice and sauce kind of place. Somewhere special with the napkins and wine and waitresses who made a career of their job. He wanted to spoil Ellie. And himself. It'd been a very long time since he'd gone upmarket for just about anything. There hadn't been the inclination because he hadn't had anyone he wanted to share that with. Taking Ellie's elbow, he led her across the road, dodging jumbos and cars, and into the outdoor area of the restaurant.

So much for a quick meal and a couple of beers, then returning to the clinic. So much for not spending too much time with Ellie and getting himself all out of sorts.

When he'd ordered a bottle of wine and they'd perused the menu and given their orders, Luca leaned back in his chair and stretched his legs under the table. 'Are you going to do any tripping around after you finish with the clinic?'

'I'd like to, but I haven't made any plans yet. Have you gone further afield than Vientiane and its surrounds?'

'No. I've been a real stay-at-home kind of guy, always finding things to do with the kids.' Travel hadn't been big on his list of things to do once he'd qualified as a doctor, and now that he was in Indochina nothing had changed. 'I'm probably wasting a golden opportunity.'

'I hear Luang Prabang is wonderful.'

'Some of the nurses who were here in June came back raving about it. You should go. It's only about an hour's flying time from here.'

Their wine arrived and Ellie sipped, her expression thoughtful.

'Something wrong with the wine? I can order

another one.' He raised his glass to his lips to taste it.

Ellie's eyes locked on him. 'Come with me.'

'What?' he spluttered into his glass.

'Let's go to Luang Prabang together. It'd be a whole lot more fun going with you. I don't fancy joining tours to see everything and then not having anyone to say do you remember to.' Her eyes were imploring him to agree.

He didn't want to disappoint her. Not at all. Besides it was way past time to get out there and see the country. 'You're on.' He could take a few days. Mid-December wasn't any busier or quieter than the rest of the year and Aaron had been nagging him to take a break.

'That's fabulous.' Her smile was worth everything. Warm and exciting, it wove through him, lifting the tension hovering in his body forever, making him want to laugh out loud.

Instead, he put down his glass and reached for her hands. With her fingers linked between his, he said, 'Thank you for giving me the kick in the backside I've been needing. It's too easy staying here pretending I'm too busy to take time out for myself.'

'I'm glad you're coming with me.' Her smile widened. 'We'll have to go after I've finished my contract.'

'That's not a problem. I'll warn Aaron tomorrow and then we can go online to make some bookings.' Flights, hotel rooms—as in plural. They wouldn't be sharing a room, a bed. The tension returned. He had to be sick in the head. Or looking out for his heart. He didn't do long-term relationships. He had his father's genes but he'd learned something growing up. Best to know his faults and act accordingly, which meant love 'em and leave 'em. He was not loving and leaving Ellie. Leaving might turn out to be impossible for starters. As for loving her? Best not to go there. He didn't want to wake up one morning to find he had a complete family around him, knowing he would one day walk out and break their hearts as he went. Yeah, he'd seen it all, knew the hurt it had caused his mum and sister, and himself, and could say he never wanted to do that to anyone. Especially not to

Ellie. But what he hadn't figured into the equation was how much he could love her, and how deep it cut not to act on that.

To think he'd agreed to go away with her. Two nights would be like two months in her company and unable to follow through on the longing he felt for her.

Ellie leaned back to allow the waitress room to put her plate down. 'Yum.' She sniffed the air and grinned. 'I wonder if I can take a local chef home to Auckland with me.'

'Are you looking forward to living in Auckland again?' he asked before forking prawns and rice into his mouth.

Her grin faded. And he felt chilled. He should never have asked. If he'd spoiled the night he only had himself to blame.

'It's going to be different. Last time you were there, as well as the other two in the house. I knew everyone training with us, whereas now I don't really know anyone up there. I'm sure I'll bump into people I used to know eventually. I do like Auckland and the job should be good.' She pushed rice around her plate. 'And it's at the other end of the North Island to where Freddy's living.'

'You'll miss him?' Was she still in love with the man?

'Not at all.' Her eyes met his and she said, 'Promise.' Finally she managed to get some rice into her mouth. When she had swallowed she added, 'I'll be able to relax. I won't be bumping into him at work or downtown. I never seemed to be able to get completely away from him. Not that either of us wanted time together, but at the hospital if we were even on the same floor people would be watching us, waiting to see if we yelled at each other—which we didn't. Not in public anyway, and then it was me doing the yelling. Not Freddy.' The spark of excitement had gone out of her eyes.

'That must've been hell. Having people watching you all the time, I mean.' Ellie tended to be a private person except with close friends and family.

'It was. So yes, Auckland's looking good. And who knows? I might decide to stay there permanently if I get another position when this next one runs out.' Sounded as if she was trying to convince herself.

If Ellie was in Auckland he'd be very tempted to return home. Where was the contract for Cambodia? He needed to sign it now before he gave in to temptation.

Temptation was staring him in the face right that moment. Ellie licking sticky rice from her fingers, then her tongue caught up a grain from the corner of her mouth. And his groin tightened exponentially. Goddamn. They were only half-way through dinner. How could he eat a thing now?

By picking up your fork and putting food in your mouth. Close your mouth—you're looking like a thirteen-year-old in lust with your teacher. Chew the damned prawn, and don't dribble.

He shuffled his butt on the chair, aiming to make everything more comfortable, and only succeeding in making his erection more appar-ent—thankfully only to himself. He was that teenaged boy all over again. The difference being Ellie was his age and not ten years older and wiser. They were both grown-ups and there was nothing to stop them having sex together. Nothing.

Except friendship and the future.

'More wine?' Ellie asked, holding the empty bottle up.

'Sure.' Might as well overindulge. The evening was already going pear-shaped fast. He nodded at the waitress across the room and leaned back, easing his legs further under the table in an attempt to shift the pressure between his legs. Pear-shaped? He nearly laughed. Not at all.

'Am I missing something here?' Ellie asked. 'You seem to be having a private joke.'

Oh, damn. Forgot she never missed a damned thing. 'You want dessert?'

Those hazel eyes locked on to his, the flecks now green and brown. Her tongue was back to its antics, tracking first along her bottom lip and then over the top one. 'Dessert? As in?'

'As in fresh fruit salad or apple pudding.'

Her tongue disappeared. Her gaze didn't. 'Right. Not as in hopping into bed and finding out exactly where we're headed?'

The shock that ricocheted through his body,

crashed into his brain, was reflected back at him from those piercing eyes. He'd swear she hadn't meant to say that. Not at all.

The wine arrived. Perfect timing, or not. Their glasses were suddenly full once more. In need of a huge gulp, Luca reached for his, slopped wine over the edge and onto his hand. He was quick to reach for his napkin to wipe his hand, not needing Ellie to lift his hand anywhere near her mouth and that tongue—if she was that way inclined, and right now he had no idea what she was thinking.

Her cheeks were pink, her gaze had shifted to a spot in the middle of the table and her glass shook when she raised it to those lips that seemed to have stolen his sanity and left him with the biggest hard-on he could remember.

Luca tugged his wallet from his back pocket and peeled out some notes, tossed them on the table, snatched up the wine bottle and got to his feet. Reaching for Ellie's hand, he said, 'Let's go.'

Her hand was warm in his. 'Where to?'

Good point. The chances of no one noticing

them sharing a room back at the clinic were next to none. 'We'll find a hotel room.'

'Sounds sleazy.' She giggled. 'But I think I might like sleazy.'

'Why is every hotel full tonight of all nights?' Luca growled as his frustration increased forty minutes later. It was all very well that there was some big festival on, but they only wanted one bed, one room. Hell, they'd give it back in a few hours.

Ellie leaned her head against his shoulder. 'Guess we'll have to run the gauntlet at home, then.'

'Taxi,' Luca yelled at a vehicle moving off from the other side of the road. 'Wait.'

He was taking Ellie to bed tonight. Nothing would stop this incessant need clawing through his body except making love with El. Nothing. He knew common sense and logic had taken a hike, knew that tomorrow he might regret this, but he had to have Ellie, had to know her better than he ever had before. Ellie was his friend, his sidekick, his—

Say it and you're doomed. Lost forever, to live

a life of purgatory, always wondering and missing out, never to be even Ellie's friend. For tonight he had to live in the moment. Not look to the future, not think back on his past. Tonight was about tonight, about him and Ellie and the sexual tension that had been simmering between them from her first day in Laos.

He held open the taxi's door. 'Let's go.'

CHAPTER EIGHT

BESIDE ELLIE IN the taxi Luca leaned forward and swore. 'Looks as if every light in the whole damned place is on.'

Ellie stared out of the side window as they drove up to the clinic. 'What's going on? The children's ward is lit up like Christmas.' She was reaching for her door handle even before the driver stopped. Her heart thudded in her chest, this time with concern for the children, not with lust and need for Luca. How quickly things changed. Though she was still hot for him her need had taken a sideways step, waiting for that moment until they found out what was happening and could hopefully get back to their evening.

They ran inside, heading straight to the ward. 'What's with all this water?' Ellie gasped.

There were people everywhere, mopping,

sweeping waves of water through the ward, removing sodden bedding. The children were helping as best they could and getting blissfully soaked as they did.

'Burst water main in the wall,' the physiotherapist told them as she squeezed a mop into a bucket. 'Not sure what happened but there was a big bang and the wall literally blew out, forcing concrete blocks outward. Pogo's bed took the full force and she's in Theatre now with a stoved-in chest from where one block slammed into her corner first.'

Ellie looked around, spied Noi and went to ask, 'Are either Luca or I needed in Theatre?'

Noi shook his head. 'No, Aaron and Louise have got it under control. One of the hospital doctors is there with them. Aaron said if you got back while they were operating you could help in here.'

Luca stood beside her. 'No problem. Any other kids need medical attention?'

'No. They're soaked and their beds are useless but no one else was hurt.'

Relieved at that, Ellie tossed her bag onto a

shelf and grabbed a mop. Turning, she bumped into Luca, felt that hard body aligned with hers. Unfortunately this was not how, only minutes ago, she'd envisaged having him against her. 'I'm sorry.'

His finger on her chin lifted her head. 'Me, too. Very sorry.'

'We might get finished cleaning up before daybreak.' How pathetic. She was almost pleading with him to take her to his room. But her disappointment was so enormous, so debilitating she wasn't thinking straight, was putting her own needs before those of the children. She should be ashamed. She was, and she wasn't. But she knew the children would win out. They had to, and she really didn't mind. But why tonight? Why couldn't that blasted pipe have burst tomorrow? Or yesterday? Or not at all?

Luca's finger brushed her bottom lip, sending sparks right down to her centre. 'We'll be lucky to get this dried out and ready for the kids before the end of the week.' His disappointment gleamed out at her from those steely eyes.

'I know.' When she'd finally decided to go for

it with him and to hell with the consequences they'd been stopped in their tracks. Was it a portent? And if it was should she heed it? At this moment she could not find it in her to say yes. She wanted Luca. 'If only there'd been one hotel with a bed to spare.'

Luca's chuckle was flat. 'If only.'

'Right. Let's get cracking. We're needed and that's got to be good, even if I wish I was somewhere else.' Ellie slopped through water to the far side of the ward where everyone was tackling the flood. 'It seems the more you're all mopping up, the more that comes out of the wall.'

Noi shook his head. 'The plumber only found the mains tap outside to turn off five minutes ago, and then it was rusted open. The water should stop any second.'

'Where are the children going to sleep until this room is habitable again?' Luca asked.

'The hospital is making room for them,' Noi answered. 'They'll be placed in various rooms with other patients.'

'I hope Pogo's going to be all right.' Ellie shivered despite the warm temperature. 'She's already had enough to deal with for a little girl.'

'A crushed rib cage is no picnic,' Luca agreed as he swept water towards the open doors that led outside. 'She was due to go home on Friday.'

Ellie squeezed her mop through the wringer on the bucket and dropped it back in the water to soak up more. Just went to show that you never knew what was around the corner. One minute Pogo was getting ready to go home, the next she was in Theatre undergoing major surgery.

One minute I was on my way to bed with Luca, the next I'm mopping a floor in the children's ward.

Kind of told her she should grab every opportunity that came along—the ones she wanted anyway. And she definitely wanted Luca. Even as she swept up water she watched him. The muscles in his arms flexed as he lifted a sodden mattress off a bed. Her mouth dried. Ironic given the amount of water around the place. She smiled. Luca did that to her.

'I'll take your bucket to empty.' Noi swung it

away and placed an empty one in front of her. 'Sorry your night was interrupted.'

Ellie gaped at him. Did he know? 'It doesn't matter, Noi. Not that this is your fault.'

'I know, but you and Luca seem to be getting on better than your first day.' He flicked looks between her and Luca.

He didn't know where they'd been headed. Relief lifted her spirits. 'That's because we've always been such good friends. I know we lost each other for a while but that friendship was strong, and still is.'

Noi turned his full attention on her. 'Friendship is good. Love is better. You know what I mean.' He wasn't asking, he was telling her.

'Aren't you meant to be emptying that bucket?' *I don't love Luca. Not like that. Not as the man I'd want to marry and have a family with.*

Noi didn't move, his gaze still fixed on her. 'He's different now. Happier and more playful with the kids since you arrived. As if you've made him come alive.'

For a man from a totally different culture from hers he seemed to understand a lot about this.

Too much. 'I didn't know he'd been unhappy.' Luca was always happy, though she'd come to realise these past weeks that had often been a front.

'So were you when you got here. Not now,' Noi said, the seriousness in his voice drumming his words into her.

Of course she'd been unhappy, in fact downright upset, distressed and incapable of moving forward. But to have got past that in such a short time? Not likely. The pain and anger was too much to evaporate so quickly. She bent to push the mop through the water, sent a wave heading across the room. 'Let's get this job finished so we can help the kids settle into their new beds.'

Noi nodded and strolled away, totally unfazed by the storm of emotions he'd started rolling through her.

What a night. She had enjoyed having dinner with Luca in a special restaurant, and appreciated the change from their usual haunts with other staff. Just sitting with him talking about things only they knew about had been relaxing. There'd been no sting in anything he'd said to her, and she hadn't felt the need to defend herself about anything. He accepted her for who she was. It was something she did not want to risk losing again.

Which meant no sex. That would put the risk factor right up there. She had no idea what the morning after would be like. Would she be able to walk away and believe they had had their moment and could return to normal? Or would she wake up and know she'd made a mistake? Realise that it had been too soon after her failed marriage and that she was probably using him to get back on her feet? Rebound sex. Rebound love.

Ellie gasped. Love? No, not that.

'You okay?' the man distracting her from the clean-up asked as he placed a bucket between them.

'Why wouldn't I be?' she growled. Rebound or not, loving Luca was not on. She couldn't love him because— Because she couldn't. It wouldn't feel right to love her best friend. Why not? He was a man, sexy as they came, kind and caring, knew her well, too well at times. There'd be no surprises. That wasn't an issue. She'd had a surprise with Freddy and look where that had got her. Single and here, debating about her feelings for Luca.

'You're pushing water in the wrong direction.' Luca grinned. 'I like it when you're muddled.'

'I don't.' *I can't love him. Not like that. Do I want to set up house with Luca? Be with him day in, day out? Have his babies? Does my heart race whenever I'm near him? My heart races—with desire. Set up house with Luca? I doubt it.* As for babies, she didn't want Luca's or anyone's. She wasn't ready. So, not love, then.

Her head shot up and she stared at him. Really stared, seeing his face, those beautiful grey eyes, that nose that had been broken when he was a kid and bent slightly to the left, that stubborn chin. She hoped not anyway. She'd loved Freddy and this felt different. *Yeah, and look where that got you.*

Noi nudged her. 'Here's your bucket.'

When she dragged her eyes sideways she found Noi nodding slowly. 'Like I said,' he added with a quick glance at Luca.

Ellie turned to run out of the room, and noticed all the people busy trying to clean up the mess and knew she wasn't going anywhere. She had to remain here, doing her share. As much as she wanted to escape and find solitude while she absorbed this new information her mind had thrown up, she couldn't. Leaving when she was needed wasn't in her psyche. So she pushed the mop harder than ever and became totally focused on water and the floor, working twice as hard as anyone else. But every time she looked up she got an eyeful of a wet and gorgeous Luca happily cleaning up the ward, teasing the kids, laughing when they tipped water over him once.

And she'd compared him to Freddy? No way. Her ex would've said to call him when everything was back to order; he wouldn't have picked up a mop. He was a surgeon, not a cleaner.

Gulp. Ellie dropped her gaze to the job in hand. Maybe she'd never really, deeply, loved Freddy at all. So what were these feelings for Luca? Friendship or love?

There was a holiday atmosphere in the clinic the next morning. The kids were hyper after their exciting night, acting as though the whole incident had been put on for their benefit.

Luca scratched his unshaven chin as he tried to eyeball every kid at the long table. 'You still have to have massages and go to school,' he told them over breakfast.

'Good luck with that,' Ellie quipped as she dumped her plate in the sink.

He needed a lot of luck with quite a few things at the moment. Like sorting out what was going on between him and Ellie. Last night they'd come so close to changing their relationship forever. So close. He was still trying to work out how he felt about that.

Sure, he'd wanted to make love with her. No question. He still did. His body had throbbed half the night with the need to touch her, to caress that soft skin, to be inside her. But this morning, in the harsh light of day, his brain had started throwing up some serious thoughts. Like, even with Ellie he had to remember his gene pool and the likelihood he'd be a bad husband and father. Like that Ellie hadn't had time to get over Freddy yet, and that *he'd* probably take the brunt of that when she came to her senses.

'I'm going to see Pogo,' Ellie announced, as though needing to make it clear she was working. Trying to combat leftover emotions from last night?

Had she had a change of heart? Finally decided last night's disaster in the clinic had been a good thing, that it had run interference before she'd had time to think everything through fully? In some ways he could agree. But a huge part of him mourned not having had that opportunity to make love with Ellie. Something in the dark recesses of his mind seemed to be saying she might be the best thing for him, might be the one woman he could risk his heart to. She certainly was nothing like Gaylene, wouldn't deny him his child—even one he thought he didn't want. Whatever it was, he shut it down immediately. Shoved to his feet and stomped across to the sink to rinse his cup and plate.

But his gaze fixed on Ellie as she left the dining hall: her head high, her shoulders tense, her hands clenched at her sides. Exhaustion after the eventful night? Or something deeper? Him? Them and what they hadn't managed to do?

He knew the feeling all too well. Throw in confusion and a need that seemed to be growing every day and he was toast.

'Can we play cricket today?' one of the boys called to him.

'Yes, of course.' That should fill in a few hours.

'Luca.' Ellie stood in front of him an hour later as he was instructing a boy on caring for his wound where he'd lost two fingers.

'Hey, Pogo's not doing so well, I hear.'

Her mouth turned down. 'No, poor wee girl. I've been sitting with her after changing bandages and adjusting her meds. Her parents are with her now.'

'They'll be gutted. Only two days ago they were saying how excited they were Pogo was going home.'

'We need to talk.' Ellie's eyes were wide as she looked at him.

His heart sank. He didn't want this conversation, would prefer to carry on as though last night hadn't nearly happened. 'About last night?'

Her smile was wobbly. 'Sort of. We are going to Luang Prabang, remember?'

How could he forget? Two nights away with Ellie and knowing now that they really shouldn't have sex if they wanted to remain friends. Oh, yeah, he remembered all right. 'Are we still on?' he asked, aware that she must say yes. *Please.*

'I hope so. We need to make bookings—for flights and a hotel.' Her cheeks turned a delicious shade of pink.

He nearly reached out to run a finger down one of those cheeks, only just in time thinking better of it. That would be an intimate gesture and he wasn't sure where he stood today. With her—or with his own thoughts. 'Want me to do them? I've got time now.'

She nodded. 'That'd be great. Do you know anyone here who could recommend accommodation?'

'Aaron and Louise went up there six months ago. I'll check with them. Two rooms, right?'

The pink deepened as she nodded. 'I guess that would be sensible.'

The last thing he felt like being was sensible. He'd done sensible all his life and lately he found it was getting tedious. But this was Ellie he was thinking of breaking the rules with and she could get hurt. That was the last thing he wanted to happen. 'What are you doing after Luang Prabang?' She'd be a free agent then. Her contract at the clinic was due to finish soon and her new one back home didn't start until the New Year. There was plenty of time for her to indulge in travelling around Indochina if she wanted. Or even stop off in Australia, as she'd mentioned one day when they were talking about one of their old housemates who'd moved to Perth.

'I'm going home.'

That was not the answer he was expecting. His surprise must've shown because she explained.

'I keep thinking there are loose ends back there that I need to deal with. I have to pack my gear and move out of Renee's apartment. Spend some time with Mum and Dad before Christmas.' A troubled look came into her eyes at the mention of her parents. Or was that Christmas?

'Seems to me you're making excuses for not staying over here longer. None of those things are going to fill in the nearly four weeks until you start work in Auckland. You don't even have to find a house up there—you've got one fully furnished for the duration.' Did she want to get as far away from him as possible?

'I could go for a coffee break right now.'

Luca took her elbow. To hell with being careful and wary. His friend appeared lost today and he'd step up to the mark for her no matter what it cost him. 'Come on. Coffee out under the tree.' Where hopefully no one would disturb them.

'I'm struggling with not knowing what I want to do,' Ellie told him ten minutes later as she sat down on the grass, not at all concerned about the ants that might bite her.

'The Ellie I remember always knew what she wanted to do about everything.'

'Right up until my marriage fell apart. Then I focused on dealing with that and the shame that followed me around. I was determined to get away from Wellington and the hospital, and here I am.' Her hands were tight around her mug.

'With the first six months of next year sorted. That can't be too bad, can it?' There were things she wasn't telling him, he just knew it, but was reluctant to ask for fear she'd walk back inside.

'Then what do I do? Work in an emergency department? Buy a house, and if so where? Even travel doesn't excite me, and I've always thought I'd do that when I had time. Pathetic.' Her sigh was long and filled with despair.

The urge to wrap her in a hug was huge but Luca sensed she wasn't ready. 'You're not pathetic, so stop feeling sorry for yourself. You've been knocked sideways by your ex, and lost sight of those plans you had with him. Of course you're confused about where you're headed.'

'I'm over here with so many places to visit, and beyond going to Luang Prabang with you I can't find the enthusiasm.' She sipped the coffee, staring at her feet.

'Give yourself time.' She was enthused about going away with him for two nights? His heart melted at the thought. He wasn't on the 'get rid of' list, then. 'They say it takes a couple of years to get over a breakup.'

'I wonder if *they* know what they're talking about.' She wrinkled her nose.

'Want to look at where you could go to after our jaunt north? Hanoi's not far from Luang Pra- bang.'

'You think I could do that on my own?'

'Asks the woman who did a solo parachute jump because she was dared? I reckon there's nothing in this world you can't do if you want to.'

Finally Ellie lifted her head and gave him the full benefit of a big smile, one that reached her eyes. 'Thank you for that. It was my turn to need a kick in the backside. You book Luang Prabang and I'll make a decision about where I'm going after that.' She placed her hand on his thigh for balance as she stood up. 'Watch this space.'

They were back to being friends, easy with each other. 'Thank goodness,' he muttered even as disappointment rippled through him. He wanted more. He knew that now. Last night hadn't been about just one night at all. But was he prepared to risk it?

No. He could get hurt, but, worse, he'd def- initely hurt El somewhere along the way. No doubt about it.

CHAPTER NINE

ELLIE'S CONTRACT WAS UP, and she and Luca were in Luang Prabang. Over the weeks she'd survived the temptation of Luca by keeping frantically busy with the children. Now they were visiting the bear sanctuary on a day trip out from the town, which had been a priority for her. 'I want to set them free,' she muttered to Luca as she clicked her camera nonstop getting photos of the black bears behind the wire fences set in the lush vegetation near the Kuang Sii waterfalls.

'I know what you mean. It seems cruel to keep them enclosed but they'll be killed if they're not protected. Catch twenty-two, I guess.'

'What I don't get is why anyone would want to hunt them in the first place. They're so beautiful.'

'As we've both said often, this is a very different world from the one we're used to.' Luca was holding his camera to his eye. 'Look at me. And smile, woman. I'm not pulling your teeth out.'

'Have you got one of the bears in the photo?' she asked.

'The bear's smiling. Now will you?'

It wasn't hard; despite the ever-present tension in her stomach brought on by all things Luca, she was having fun. Not even thinking about what she might be missing out on sleeping in separate rooms at the hotel could wipe her smile away. They'd been on the go since arriving yesterday.

'At last,' Luca growled and clicked a photo. And another, and another until she shifted away. 'I could sell them on the internet.'

'Good luck.' She laughed. 'The guide's beckoning—guess it's time to head back.'

'A cold beer would go down a treat.' Luca smacked his lips. 'This humidity's getting to me.'

'They sell it at the stalls where the van's parked.' She wouldn't mind one, either. She slipped her arm through his. 'Let's check them out before we go. Bye-bye, bears.'

'You're dribbling, and I haven't got anything to wipe your slobber up with.'

With beers in hand they clambered into the van to join the three Australian guys sharing the trip. Ellie stretched her legs towards the door and leaned back in her seat to enjoy the terrain they'd pass through. 'Next stop, Elephantville.'

The weather turned wet about the time they climbed off the elephant they'd ridden through the jungle. Rushing under the shelter, where there were bananas to feed the animals, Ellie felt the sweat trickle down her back. 'The rain doesn't stop the humidity, does it?'

Luca shoved his camera into a plastic bag and put it inside his day bag. 'Give it time.'

Suddenly the rain became torrential, pounding the tin roof of the shelter and making conversation next to impossible.

Ellie leaned close to Luca to yell, 'Wonder how long this will last.'

'Who knows?' he yelled back, then jerked his head back.

'Luca?' He hadn't shaved that morning and a dark stubble highlighted his strong jawline—

and sent waves of something suspiciously like desire rolling through her. What would he do if she ran a finger over his chin?

'Let's go. The driver's waving us over to the van.' He raced away, stomping through puddles, getting soaked from all directions.

Not that there was any choice. Ellie braced herself for the drenching she was about to get and chased after him, wondering at his abrupt mood swing.

'The skies are angry.' The driver laughed as he slammed his door. 'We have muddy ride back.'

Ellie felt a prickle of apprehension. The road hadn't been that great when it was dry. Her hand slid sideways, onto Luca's thigh. His fingers laced around hers and he squeezed gently.

'We'll be fine. This guy will be used to driving in these conditions. They're not uncommon up here in the hills, from what the man at the hotel said this morning.'

'I guess.' The apprehension backed off but she didn't withdraw her hand, enjoying the way Luca's forefinger rubbed across her knuckles. *Please don't pull away. Not yet.* Heat sparked along the veins of her arm. Eek, if having her hand held by Luca did this to her, what would making love be like? She suspected like nothing she'd ever experienced.

On the ride up out of the valley the van slipped and slid on the mud and water pouring down the road. The sound of the wheels spinning filled the van. Ellie wondered if they'd have been better waiting until the deluge slowed, but when she'd voiced that opinion the driver replied, 'Might not stop for days.'

Her grip tightened around Luca's hand. Her jaw ached as her teeth clenched. Leaning against him, she found some comfort even though there was nothing he could do if this trip went badly. Luca's jaw was jutting out, his eyes not wavering from the road ahead. The van was quiet, everyone probably holding their breath as she was.

Then suddenly they popped over the crest of the hill and the van tilted forward as they headed down. The relief was palpable, until everyone realised going down had its own set of problems. The driver braked repeatedly to slow the van but they skidded more often than on the way up.

When the van slid towards the edge of the road Ellie thought she must be breaking the bones in Luca's fingers, her grip was so tight. She tasted blood on her lip where her teeth pushed down. The air stuck in her lungs, her ribs tight under the pressure. 'Oh, no. We're going over the edge. We're going to crash.'

Up front the driver was shouting something incomprehensible as he spun the steering wheel left, then right.

And the van slid closer to the top of the ravine.

A scream filled Ellie's throat, but when she opened her mouth nothing came out.

Luca's hand was strong around hers. His body tense beside her. 'Jeez.' Then he let her go to grab at the latch that was the internal handle on the sliding door. His muscles stood out as he strained to tug the door back on its rollers. His lips pressed together until there was no colour in them. And still he pulled, frantically trying to open the door.

Nothing happened.

The back of the van lurched forward with a thud. The wheels were over the edge.

Ellie's heart stopped.

This was it. The van would drop like a boulder to the bottom of the ravine. *We're going to die.* Ellie jerked in her seat, staring around, frantic for a way out.

Slam. The noise was horrendous. Air whooshed inside.

'Come on,' Luca yelled as he grabbed her arm. 'Jump.'

The door was open. That had been the slamming sound.

'Jump, Ellie. Now.'

She didn't get a chance. Even as she strained against the steepening angle of the van Luca snatched at her, wrapped his arms around her and fell out backwards.

Thump. They landed heavily on the side of the bank. Pain tore through Ellie's side where her hip had connected with something solid and unforgiving. The air whooshed out of her lungs. Her head snapped back, crashed against the ground. Luca's arms were no longer holding her. She cried out, 'Luca?' Then she gasped in air, tried again. 'Luca, where are you?' He had better be all right. She couldn't imagine what she'd do if anything had happened to him.

'El, I'm here. Are you okay?'

She'd never heard such a beautiful sound. 'Yes, I think so. Are you?'

Her relief was snatched away by a loud bang and the noise of metal being torn and bent. The van had come to a halt wrapped around a tree.

'The driver, the Aussies. Luca—' The words dried up on her tongue. They didn't have a chance of surviving that crash.

A familiar, warm hand gripped her shoulder. 'We'll get help.' That hand was shaky. 'Are you sure you're all right?'

Pain thudded through her hip but when she shifted her leg nothing felt broken. She nodded. 'Thanks to you.' Twisting her head, she kissed the back of Luca's hand. 'What about you?'

'A few bruises but think I got lucky.'

'You're not lying? Not going all macho on me?' When Luca shook his head Ellie began pushing herself up to the road, sliding in the mud as she made hard work of the short distance. Her body was shaking as if she had the DTs. Shock did that, she knew. She concentrated hard, thought about the situation. 'What are the chances of another vehicle coming along in this weather?'

Luca was right behind her. 'That tourist bus was due to leave right after us. Though how a bus will manage on that road when the van was struggling, I don't know.'

Ellie shuddered. A busload of people going over the edge didn't bear thinking about. 'Wait. I hear something.' She strained to listen through the torrential rain.

'Not a bus but a four-wheel drive, I'm thinking.' Luca stepped into the middle of the road, slip-sliding in the mud and waving wildly. 'Hell, not one but three of them. We just got lucky, El.'

Guess luck was relative. Guilt assailed her. They *were* lucky. There were four people still in that mangled van down the bank. The only luck for them was she and Luca were doctors, doctors with nothing but their bare hands and the knowledge in their heads. If they were still in need of medical intervention.

'You're not going down there,' Luca informed

her moments later in a do-not-argue-with-me tone. 'It's too dangerous.'

'Right, I'm to stand up here watching you risking your life? I don't think so.' She turned to find people from the vehicles now parked to the side of the road approaching with ropes.

'El,' Luca growled. 'Two of these men are going down with me. If we can get anyone out of the van, the others will pull them up here for you to attend to.' Again his hand was on her shoulder, his fingers gently squeezing. 'There won't be an ambulance turning up. It's up to all of us to get these people stabilised and to a hospital.' His voice was calm, encouraging, not like that of someone who'd barely escaped with his life minutes earlier.

Shame at her outburst had her apologising. The last thing Luca needed right now was a hysterical female on his shaky hands. 'Sorry. You're right. Again. But, Luca, please be careful.' She couldn't lose him now. Even as a friend he was too precious to her. She'd lost enough people this past year for various reasons.

'Promise.'

Standing around waiting, peering over the edge and sucking a deep breath every time one of the men slipped, which was often, nearly drove her nuts. She only let the breath go when she knew for sure that man was all right. When Luca slid down a steep, muddy patch too fast her heart slammed her ribs. 'You promised you'd be careful,' she whispered. 'I should've asked you to promise that you'd be safe and not get hurt.'

'Over here,' a male voice called through the gloom from halfway down the slope.

Luca and another guy veered off to the right, and very soon were crouched beside a small bush where what Ellie finally recognised as feet were sticking out from.

Soon Ellie's first patient had been hauled up to the road and she had something to keep her mind off Luca. The guy was caked in mud and muck, soaked through from the rain, and still managed to crack a joke. 'Didn't read this bit on the tourist brochure. Must've caught the wrong ride.'

Hot tears filled Ellie's eyes and she had to blink rapidly to dispel them. 'You and the rest of us. You want to tell me where you're hurt so I can check you out?'

'I don't need to be hurting for you to do that, babe. Been eyeing you up all morning.'

'I'm a doctor,' she told him. His face was pale underneath the mud that was slowly washing off in the rain. 'Let's get you into one of the vehicles. Don't see why we need to be getting any more drenched than we already are.'

A man she hadn't noticed standing nearby put a hand under the Aussie guy's elbow. 'Here, lean against me.'

The Aussie was limping and he held the other arm tight against his chest. 'Thanks, mate. Think my arm's broken.'

After slitting the sleeve up with a pocketknife the other man handed her, Ellie noted a large swelling over the tibia that suggested her patient was right. 'I'll create a makeshift sling so that you don't move or jar your arm until you're in hospital.' When and where that was she had no idea. 'What else? You were limping.'

'Everything seems to be working. Think my thigh hit something hard when I was thrown out of the van. Probably only bruised, though it hurts like a bitch.'

Yeah, Ellie could commiserate. Nor was her hip happy, protesting every time she bumped against the door or moved sharply. 'Let's take a look.'

More vehicles stopped, more people slid down the bank to help extricate the driver and the other two passengers. Luca finally returned to the road and helped Ellie do whatever she could for the injured men. One by one they were taken away in various vehicles, heading for proper medical care. The driver remained unconscious throughout the whole ordeal of being pulled free of his stoved-in van and hauled up the bank. With no oxygen or monitors of any description Ellie and Luca did their best to make him comfortable before seeing him off in a truck that had just turned up.

'I'll give you two a lift into Luang Prabang,' one of the first men to stop told them. 'You look knackered.'

That would be an understatement, Ellie admitted to herself. Sore, soaked through, muddy and still shaking, she desperately wanted a hot shower.

Luca held her hand all the way back to their hotel. Tightly. They were both shivering from cold and fright. Though the temperature was as hot and the air as muggy as ever, Ellie couldn't believe the chills tightening her skin. Her saturated clothes clung to her, pulling at her skin every time she moved.

At the hotel entrance she tugged off her canvas shoes before going inside, but she still left a trail of footprints and water as she crossed to the stairs leading up to where their rooms were situated. Luca still held her hand, his shoes swinging from the fingers of his other one.

They hardly uttered a word all the way, and even when Ellie tried again and again to shove the key into the lock, Luca said nothing. He merely took the key from her shaking hand and tried three times before he succeeded. He followed her into her room, dropped his shoes on the mat and headed for the bathroom. 'You need out of those clothes and under the shower, like now.'

'So do you.' She was already unbuckling the belt on her trousers, then pushing them down her legs, the wet fabric clinging to her skin.

The sound of running water came from the bathroom. 'Give that a few seconds to warm up.' Luca stood in front of her.

Ellie stopped struggling with her T-shirt and stared up at this wonderful man who'd just been through hell with her. For all the moisture she carried in her clothing and her hair, her mouth was dry. 'That was way too close.'

His eyes widened in agreement as he reached for the hem of her shirt and started to lift it up over her breasts and then her head. 'Yes, it was.'

She shuddered. And slipped her arms up so as he could get her shirt off. Her hands joined behind his neck, pulling his head closer to hers. 'We're alive.'

'Yep.' His lips brushed hers. 'And wet and shivering.' He scooped her up into his arms and headed for the bathroom and all that glorious warm steam that was now beginning to fill the tiny room. One arm was around her back with his hand on her lace-covered breast, the other arm under her knees with his fingers splayed across the top of one knee. Heat filled her, banishing the chills, even where Luca's wet shirt clung to her rib cage. Need poured through her, need to prove she was alive and well, need for Luca.

Setting her down in the shower box, he began unzipping his shorts. 'Move over.'

She didn't need a second invitation. Scuttling sideways, she reached for him, pulled him into the shower even before he'd finished undressing. Gently wiping the mud off his cheeks, his neck, his arms, she felt him unclasp her bra at her back.

Luca pushed her thong down, his hands taking it past her thighs, over her knees and down to her ankles, where he lifted one foot then the other to free the thin scrap of lace. Upright again, those strong hands she adored touching her gripped her buttocks. 'We're alive, El. And I'm going to prove how much.' Then he lifted her so she could wrap her legs around his waist.

Her mouth sought his, her tongue instantly inside the hot cavern of his mouth. Hot. Heat. Real.

This was real, making the blood pound through her veins, in her ears, deafening yet wonderful as the regular thumping beat the rhythm of life. *We're alive.*

Pushing her breasts hard against his chest, she rubbed back and forth, absorbing the exquisite sensations blasting her as she felt Luca's skin sliding against hers. Feeling each individual finger where he touched her backside, knowing the sensation of his palms on her soft skin. Feeling, feeling, feeling. Nothing, no one, had ever felt so wonderful, so full of promise.

Now she wanted all of him; needed to feel his length slide inside her, fill her. Then, and only then, would she truly believe they had survived. His erection was pulsing between her legs, against her opening. Ellie began to slide down over him, drawing his manhood into her, gasping with wonder at the strength and length of him. 'Luca,' she cried. She was more than ready. As the tension coiling in her stomach, at the apex of her legs, everywhere, began tightening farther, Luca tensed, then thrust upward, hard, driving into her, again and again, proving he was here, alive and well, and with her.

As the tension gripping her exploded into an orgasm Ellie screamed, 'Luca. Luca.'

'El, oh, yes. That's it. That's good.' He rode her hard and deep, and when he came his eyes snapped open to lock with hers. Eyes full of understanding and longing and bewilderment—and gratitude. For being here, and not down that ravine? For sharing this with her?

'El' was all he said as he held her tight against his body, his hands lightly rubbing her buttocks, shivering through the end of his release. 'El.' The tiniest word meaning so, so much.

They dried each other off, taking their time to discover the other's body. 'You are beautiful,' Luca whispered as he carefully ran the corner of his towel beneath her breast. The small, heavy globe filled his hand to perfection. Her nipple peaked even as he stared at it and he lowered his mouth to savour her. One swipe with his tongue and that peak tightened further. So did his penis.

Down, boy. This time they were going for long and slow and getting to know each other better.

Something like hope filtered through the postcoital haze blurring his mind. Never had he known such excitement with a woman, so much release and relief and care, so—different and special. Almost loving. Had he been driven by the need to acknowledge he'd survived a horrific crash? Or something more? Something to do with Ellie herself? Had she always been his future? Had he been blind to what was right under his nose?

His gut clenched into a tight knot. Ellie was soon leaving Laos, bound for Perth and then home. Which was a good thing; it had to be. They didn't, and couldn't, have a future other than their rekindled friendship. That was the only way he could ever continue with her in his life. The other—becoming lovers beyond today—was unthinkable, would break every rule he'd made for himself. Would open him up to his vulnerabilities. He wasn't prepared to do that. Not even for Ellie, not even to have her by his side forever. Because she was a 'forever' kind of girl. He suspected that was why she hurt so much about Freddy leaving her. The commitment she'd made to him and their marriage had been broken.

Forget her failed marriage. Right now his body was humming with after-sex lethargy and the need to repeat the whole thing. As soon as possible. His body was going in the opposite direction to his mind, and he couldn't stop it. His body, that was. Why did he say making love when with Ellie? Every other time in his life he'd had sex. When he'd driven into her, pumped his soul into her, he'd known he was safe in every way. Hell, he'd felt complete for the first time in his adult life, maybe since the day he was born. As if he'd found home, which was plain untrue. Home was where the heart was, or something like that, according to a saying out there. But his heart wasn't up for grabs. Not even Ellie was going to snag it. Though these past few weeks it'd been getting harder and harder to deny he wanted and needed her in his life on a regular basis. As in a partner. A life partner. His heart.

'Luca.' Her soft voice skidded across his skin.

'You still with me?' She dropped his towel and ran her palms over his chest, her thumbs lightly flicking his nipples and sending sparks flying out to every corner of his body. Those warm, tender palms cruised lower, over his abs, and lower.

The breath caught in his lungs.

Her hand wrapped around him. Slid down, up, down.

His brain went on strike. The time for thinking was over. His body took up the challenge. He had to have El. Again. Now. The need to taste her, to feel her hot moistness surround his desire was rampaging along his veins, through his muscles, weakening his ability to stay upright—even when his hands were fondling those beautiful breasts.

'El, I need you.' Snatching her up into his arms, he carried her the short distance to the small double bed filling the tiny room and laid her down. Had he really said that?

It's true. I did and I do.

Hopefully Ellie hadn't heard, or if she had then she'd pass it off as something he'd said in the heat of the moment. Which it was. If his brain had been in good working order he'd never have uttered those words.

Truth will out.

Yeah, so they said. He lowered himself beside Ellie and reached for her. His fingers caressed a trail from her lips to her throat to her breasts to her belly button and beyond. El.

CHAPTER TEN

'I'M STARVING.' ELLIE STRETCHED the full length of the ridiculously small bed to ease all the kinks out of her muscles. Pain erupted in her hip. 'Ow!' she cried out. 'Why didn't I feel that when we were making out?'

'Because I'm a bigger distraction?' Luca raised up onto an elbow and lifted the sheet to study her hip. 'That's a piece of work. More colours than the rainbow.' His lips were softer than a moth as they brushed over the tender surface of her beleaguered hip.

She did an exaggerated eye roll. 'Oh, please. Your ego needs controlling.'

He grinned. 'I know.' Then he turned all serious. 'Sorry I threw you onto a rock on the way out of that van.'

There was a lot behind those flippant words. He had saved them from a worse fate. Instead of freaking out in that tumbling metal box that was their transport he'd done something about the situation, done his absolute best to save them. He was her hero. She thought of the driver. 'I wonder how Palchon is. If he's regained consciousness.' *If he's alive.*

'We could go find out on our way to Luang Prabang's airport this morning.'

'I'd like that.' Ellie sat up, groaned as pain again reminded her of her hip. 'My upcoming flight to Perth is looking less exciting. Can you get me some painkillers in Vientiane, and something to help me sleep?' Not that she'd been thrilled about leaving Laos anyway. *Be honest.* It was Luca she didn't want to leave. But that shut-down look that had just appeared on his face told her more than anything that he did not want to carry this on any further. What they'd had together in this small hotel room was all they were going to have.

Her heart shattered. She loved Luca. She'd loved him as a friend, and now as a lover. But most of all she loved him as a man, for all the pieces that made him who he was. For his tenderness, for the way he had always listened to her grizzles and cheered her up when the world came tumbling down on top of her, the mess of dirty clothes he never put in the wash for days on end, his skill as a doctor. She loved him completely.

Ironic really, when she'd come to Laos to sort herself out and instead got herself caught up in love with Luca, when he'd made it plain he did not reciprocate her feelings. She'd be going home flattened and filled with despair. Home would now be in Auckland, a city filled with memories of Luca.

Unless this was love on the rebound, and then she could hope that eventually, hopefully in the not too distant future, she'd get over Luca. It was debatable whether they could ever go back to be best friends again. So whichever way this turned out, she'd lost someone else important to her. The sooner the year finished, the better. She was going to dance and drink and sing the new year in like never before, welcome it with open arms, then get on with her new job and creating the career that'd take her through the next twenty years without falter.

'I'll head back to my room to shower and pack my toothbrush.' Luca stood up from the bed in full naked glory.

'Sure.' He was beautiful. Had he always looked like this beneath his snappy shirt and fitting trousers? She'd seen him in running shorts and T-shirts, in track pants, in jeans, everything a normal well-dressed man would wear, and she'd had no idea what he was covering up. Blind? Or had she been that unaware of her feelings for him? Went to show this love thing was new, not something that had been lurking in the back of her head.

'If we're going to have breakfast and visit the hospital we need to get a shake along, Ellie.' He wrapped a towel around his waist.

'Sure,' she repeated, still drinking in the sight of toned muscles and long, strong limbs. How could she have missed those? 'See you in thirty,' she muttered through a salivating mouth.

'Make that twenty. We don't want to miss the flight back to Vientiane. Who knows when we'd get another one? We were lucky getting this one.'

And tomorrow she was heading to Australia.

Tossing back the sheet, she leaped up, ignoring the protest from her hip. Funny how that hadn't been a problem while making love with Luca. 'Twenty it is.' An exciting thought snagged her, Miss the flight and have more time in bed with Luca. But looking at his face showed that wasn't going to happen.

Slamming the bathroom door shut, she jerked the taps on and stepped under the cold water. Gasping, she crossed her arms over her breasts and gritted her teeth until the water warmed up. She tried to put aside thoughts of Luca and her new-found love and concentrate on the mundane, like getting clean, dressed, her make-up on and the few items she'd brought here back in her bag. Forget everything else for now. There were many hours in the air when she'd have nothing else to do but think. Or sleep if Luca got those sleeping pills for her.

According to the American doctor at the local hospital their van driver had regained consciousness but he wouldn't be going anywhere in a hurry. Both femurs were broken from where he'd impacted with the dashboard, and ribs had been fractured, presumably by the steering wheel as he was thrown forward.

'What happens?' Luca asked. 'Does he stay in hospital until he's back on his feet? Or will he be sent home within a day or two?'

'I'll keep him here as long as possible, but—' the man shrugged '—it won't be nearly long enough.'

'I'd like to help out financially,' Luca said quietly. 'How do I go about that?'

As Ellie listened to Luca and the other doctor discussing how to give the man's family money to see them through the next few weeks she looked around at the basic hospital emergency room. Nothing like what she'd trained in: not a lot of equipment or any up-to-date beds. There was little privacy for the patients, and families sat on the floor by their loved ones. Yet everyone seemed grateful for any attention they received. Also not like home where some patients and their families felt no compunction over telling medical staff what they expected of them.

'Right, let's go. That plane won't wait.'

That plane was delayed for nearly an hour. Sitting on a cold, hard seat, Ellie watched Luca pace up and down the departure lounge. It was as if he was busting to get back to the clinic. He sure as hell didn't have anything to say to her. He'd gone from caring, loving and sexy to cool, focused and resolute. She'd been cut off.

Beside her a baby kicked her tiny legs and made gurgling noises. Ellie turned her attention to the cutest little girl she'd ever seen and made cooing sounds. Swathed in pink clothes and blanket, the baby had to be sweltering but Mum seemed unperturbed.

'She's gorgeous,' Ellie said.

While it was obvious the mother didn't understand the words she'd picked up on Ellie's tone and smiled broadly. Nodding her head, she spoke rapidly in a language Ellie hadn't heard before. Not Laotian, for sure.

'Can I?' Ellie held her hands out, fully expecting to be rebuffed.

But the woman happily handed her precious child over, adjusting the blanket around the baby's face when Ellie settled her in her arms.

More kicks and gurgles came her way from the warm little bundle. 'What's her name?' she asked without thinking.

The mum stared at her, a question in her big brown eyes.

Ellie tapped her own chest. 'Ellie.' Then she lightly touched the baby's arm. 'Name?'

The woman said, 'Ellee?' Or something that vaguely sounded like her name. Then she tapped her chest and said, 'Sui.' Nodding at the baby, she added, 'Bubba.'

Bubba as in baby, or was that her name? Something in a foreign language that Ellie couldn't decipher? 'Bubba.' She copied the mother and grinned down at the baby.

What would it feel like to be holding her own baby like this? Her heart slowed, squeezed gently. It would be wonderful, precious. And not something that was about to happen in the foreseeable future. She didn't seem to do so well choosing the men she fell in love with. One hadn't wanted a family with her despite reassuring her in the beginning he did, and Luca didn't want a relationship with her at all, when he'd be brilliant as a dad. He didn't want a family of his own at all. Maybe she should abandon any hope for a husband and her own children. That could save a lot of heartbreak in the future. Except her heart had begun to ache for those things. With Luca.

The PA system announced their flight was ready for boarding. Ellie looked around for Luca. She stilled as she found those intense grey eyes fixed on her, flicking between her and the baby. What? Had she done something wrong? Was it not the done thing to hold another woman's baby for a few minutes? To enjoy feeling the tiny girl squirming and kicking? Whatever Luca thought, it had been a magical moment she was glad she'd taken.

Another look at Luca and she saw it—the longing fighting to get out. Luca wanted children. She'd swear it. But as she locked her gaze on his he shut her out. The blinkers were back in place and he was giving nothing away. Instead, he tipped his head in the direction of the door leading out onto the tarmac and mouthed, 'Ready?'

Handing Bubba back to her mother, Ellie said,

'Thank you for letting me hold her.' Then she put her hands, palms together, in front of her chest, nodded and said, 'Goodbye.'

The woman rewarded her with a huge smile.

A smile that Ellie wore in her heart on the hour's flight back to Vientiane. Luca might be withdrawing but she wouldn't let that dampen the feelings holding that baby had evoked. No way.

If only Luca would admit to feeling the same. About babies. About her and him.

Luca knew he was behaving badly but he didn't know how else to keep Ellie at arm's length. He was afraid that if he let her close he'd haul her into his arms and never let her leave his side.

That night in Luang Prabang should never have happened, yet he couldn't find it in himself to wish it hadn't. Making love to Ellie had been off the wall. Like nothing he'd ever experienced before. That sense of finding himself had increased when they'd gone to bed for their second intimate connection.

With Ellie he thought he probably could face

his demons and even keep them at bay. But reality sucked. Beneath the surface lurked those genes he'd inherited from his father and his mother's father. More than ever he did not want to hurt anyone when that person could be Ellie. She'd had her share of pain. She didn't need him giving her a relapse. Which was why when they'd finally got back to Vientiane yesterday he'd made himself busy at the hospital until long after Ellie had headed to her room for the night.

'You can smile.' Ellie leaned against his arm. 'Everyone else is.'

Aaron and Louise were having fun, drinking copious quantities of wine and cracking mediocre jokes. They were at a restaurant and bar, enjoying the evening despite the fact they were losing Ellie in a few hours. 'Seeing Ellie off in style' was how Louise had put it on the way into town nearly two hours earlier.

It was the nature of the clinic, people coming and going with monotonous regularity. Not many stayed for a year like him, while Louise and Aaron set the record for how long they'd been here.

'I guess our misadventure has caught up with me,' Luca murmured as his nostrils filled with that particular scent he now recognised as Ellie's. Floral without being too sweet, reminding him of the spring air back home. Reminding him of what he could not have.

'Great,' Ellie snapped, tipping her head away from him.

Hiding? Then he thought about what he'd said and shook his head. 'That wasn't a criticism of you or us or how the night unfolded. I am tired, but, more than that, I'm trying to deal with having found my best friend only to be losing her again.'

'Come on, you two. Let's all dance together one last time.' Aaron stood up and reached for Ellie's hand, but Louise took one look at Ellie and then him and dragged Aaron away, leaving them to this conversation that sucked and had no possible outcome that would please either of them.

'You haven't lost me,' Ellie argued, now back to facing him. 'We've changed the nature of our relationship but we're not breaking up.' Was that hope in her eyes?

'I've lost my friend,' he reiterated. He was being cruel to be kind. He couldn't give her anything but friendship and she appeared to want more. Lots more.

The colour drained from her cheeks as she gasped. Hurt glittered out at him from those eyes that followed him into sleep every night. 'No. You can't do that to me.'

I can't save your heart? Give me a break here. I'm thinking of you, looking out for you. 'Ellie, go home and start that new job, find an apartment or a house to make yours, give yourself time to get over your marriage and then start dating again. One mistake doesn't mean you can't find happiness again.' *Only, it won't be with me.*

Ellie lifted her glass, drained it of water and banged it back on the table. 'I don't want to lose anyone else. I just got you back.'

'We made a mistake.' At least he'd had the good sense not to realise that until after he'd learned what it was like to make love with Ellie.

He'd never forget, even if he was now spoiled forever.

'I'll tell you what a mistake is.' She held one finger up in front of him. 'Marrying a man I believed loved me enough to want to be there when I got old and grey and used a walking stick.' A second finger went up. 'Trusting Caitlin not to sleep with my husband.'

Shock stunned him. 'Your sister slept with Freddy?' He'd always believed the worst of Baldwin, but this? Luca couldn't get his head around the idea of the guy going with his wife's sister. That went way beyond bad. No wonder there was always wariness and despair lurking in Ellie's eyes. She and her sister had been close.

Ellie hadn't finished. A third finger rose, and her whole hand shook. 'Freddy loves Caitlin. Caitlin loves Freddy. They want to get married as soon as the divorce goes through.'

Luca wrapped both his hands around the one wavering in front of his face. 'El, don't torture yourself. They're the bad guys here, not you.' How did she get up every morning? When did she plaster her smiles on? Seconds before bumping into the kids waiting for her to appear outside her room at the clinic? Who did she trust these days?

Him. It struck him with blinding certainty. Ellie trusted him. *Wrong, girl, absolutely wrong.* Which was why he was fighting the churning need to take her in his arms and kiss her better, never to let her go again. To forget everything he'd been trying to tell himself moments earlier.

'I need a friend, Luca. You.' She swallowed. 'But there's more to what I'm feeling. I've always loved you as a friend.'

Don't say it. Don't. Please. It was going to hurt them both, and then he'd hurt her some more. But he couldn't look away, couldn't find the right words—if they existed—to stop her from laying out everything between them.

'My feelings for you aren't like they used to be, and yesterday kind of underlined that. Making love with you was beautiful.' She paused, staring into his eyes. Searching for what? Waiting for what? Finally, on a long, sad sigh, she continued, 'You know what I'm afraid of, Luca? That for me this is rebound love, and that I'll wake up one day and wish my friend back and my lover gone. The pain would be enormous, but I'm prepared to risk it. Because I believe you—we—are worth it. Because I'm not so sure that this isn't the real deal and what I felt for Freddy was the lesser.' Her head dropped. 'Which doesn't put me in a good light at all.'

'We all make mistakes.' Though not always as big as what this sounded like—on both sides of the marriage. 'You've got to learn to let go, El, drop all that hurt caused by Freddy and Caitlin, and then you'll see our relationship for what it is. Friendship. Nothing more. Or less.'

'You make it sound so easy.' Acid burned in her words; pain flattened her mouth.

Luca stood up, pulling Ellie up with him. He needed fresh air, to walk, to stare at the stars. To explain to El that she was so wrong about them, had got everything completely back to front. Because of what Freddy and Caitlin had done she was searching for someone to make her feel better. Sounding more and more as if her rebound theory was correct. 'Come for a walk.'

'There's not a lot of time before I have to head

to the airport.' Suddenly she sounded reluctant, as if she knew she'd gone too far.

'This won't take long.' At least it wouldn't if he could get the words out. He was afraid. Because the moment he said what had to be said he'd lose Ellie again, this time probably permanently. When he reached for her hand she stepped sideways and folded her arms as though she was cold and not avoiding him. But he knew different.

If he waited a while longer there'd be no time, and he owed her an explanation. Dread lined his stomach, making it heavy and tight. 'In Luang Prabang, that was glad-to-be-alive sex. We'd both had a huge shock, were grateful to get off that hillside in one piece, and naturally we celebrated in the most obvious way. It was great sex, the best I've ever had, but, Ellie, you must see that there's no future in it. We're friends, I care a lot for you, but nothing's changed. I still won't get married or have kids.' If he said it all fast enough it started to sound right. 'Those are the things you ultimately want in your life. Not yet. I get that it's far too soon. But I'm *never* going there.'

He was breathing fast, as if he'd run a marathon or something. His heart beat hard and erratically. As for what was going on in his head, the kaleidoscope of emotions and need mocking his words—he wasn't going there, couldn't go there. He'd hate to find he'd got this all wrong.

Ellie rounded on him, stabbed a finger at his chest. 'Aren't you going too far with your assertions that I want to marry you?'

He held his hands up. 'Just laying it all out right from the get-go. I come from a line of lousy commitment-phobes. I'm trying to save you here.'

'Pathetic.' Her hands banged onto her hips, and she winced. Must've hurt the bruised one. 'You're blaming the men in your life for your avoidance issues when deep down you want to love and be loved. You want a family of your own, but you're too damned afraid to reach out and try for that.'

'You don't know what you're talking about.'

'Really? Then, why have you only ever dated

the kind of women that won't want the whole nine yards?' Ellie turned away, turned back, her face softening as she gazed at him. 'You've proved yourself time and time again, Luca. You did everything you could for your nephew. You haven't given up on him despite his mother kicking you out of his life. I've seen you with young patients, never letting them down, always ready to stay hours longer than required to make sure they're coping.'

'That's not the same.' Why couldn't she understand he wasn't doing this for the hell of it? That, yeah, he'd like to make happy families—with her, what was more—if only there was a spitting chance in hell of it working. 'Even Angelique proved we've got bad genes by doing to Johnny what Mum did to us—refusing to acknowledge his father.'

Ellie shook her head at him and began to walk back towards the restaurant. Her time was almost up and she had to get to the airport. Luca's heart was breaking. This time was different from when they last went their separate ways. Then she'd been going to Freddy, and he'd had Gaylene on his back. He'd always believed that one day they'd get back in touch. Tonight he knew this was the end for them. 'Ellie,' he called softly. 'I'm sorry.'

She had to have supersensitive hearing because she came back to him and placed her hands gently on his cheeks. 'So am I, Luca. So am I. Do me one favour? Let go of some of that control you hold over your emotions. Start taking some risks with your heart. Stop blaming everyone else.' Reaching up on her toes, she kissed him, not with the passion of yesterday, not lightly as she used to as a friend, but as a woman who loved him and knew she'd lost him before they'd even started.

CHAPTER ELEVEN

ELLIE STARED AROUND the apartment she'd been sharing with Renee since the day she'd moved out of her marital home. 'I'm going to miss this, you, even Wellington,' she told Renee. 'But not the hospital.' Though now, after Luca, it almost seemed easier to stay here in the same city as her ex and Caitlin. At least here she had Renee and a handful of casual friends she enjoyed evenings with at five-star restaurants or going to shows.

She had this awful feeling that wherever she went her heart was going to take time to put all the pieces back together. All she could hope for was that some day way ahead she'd stop feeling this debilitating pain. Hell, she'd thought Freddy and Caitlin had hurt her. She'd had no idea.

Renee gave her a tired smile. Three gruel-ling nights with an extremely ill two-year-old requiring two emergency operations had done that to her. 'You can change your mind any time you like. Save me the hassle of finding another roomie.'

It was tempting. Running away didn't come naturally. 'I've signed a contract.'

'Six months isn't exactly long-term.' Renee never minded firing the shots directly at her target, which was why Ellie liked her so much. No bull dust. 'I'll keep your room for you that long.'

'Stop it. I might do a Luca next and go overseas, though not to Asia.' Australia or the UK appealed more at the moment.

'I still can't get my head around Luca ditching his super career and going over there for a year. Back when we were all sharing that house he drove the rest of us bonkers with his plans for running the biggest and greatest A and E department in the country.'

'That Luca's gone. Or missing in dispatches at the moment.' Whether he'd ever return to those goals she had no idea. 'He's not easy in his new skin, but I now wonder how comfortable he was in his old one.'

'Backstory. I wonder what his is. He never

talked about his family, did he? Even when we'd been on the turps and talking a load of nonsense about ourselves.' Renee looked pensive. 'Does that mean there are some nasty skeletons in his cupboard?'

'Luca definitely thinks so. Certainly lets them rule how he lives his life.' Anger rose suddenly, unexpectedly, nearly choking Ellie. He let his unknown father dominate him. He'd pushed her away because of a man he hadn't met. *Thanks a bundle, Luca.* He didn't deserve her. Yeah, way to go. Her anger deflated as quickly as it had come, replaced by sadness—and despair. 'He does have issues, but until he decides to talk them through they're not going anywhere.'

'And you? You've come home broken-hearted.' Renee handed her a mug of milky coffee even though she hadn't asked for one. 'Are you going to be okay?'

'I'm an old hand at this. At least in Auckland I won't have to put up with knowing nods and snide remarks about my model sister and how awful it must be trying to keep up with her fashion sense and stunning figure.' Ouch. *More than bitter, Ellie.*

Renee growled, 'Stop it. It's over now.' She was repeating Luca's words. 'Even if you stayed on in Wellington I think you'd find no one cares anymore. In fact I've lost count of the number of people asking me how you're getting on and when you're coming back.'

'So they can talk about me again.'

'Ellie, give it a rest. I thought you were moving on from all this, then you return from Laos all in a pickle again. If Luca's upset you, that's one thing, but to carry on about Freddy and Caitlin still is another. It's been nearly a year. Don't you think it's time to accept they are serious about their relationship? Even if they did go about it all wrong and hurt you so badly.'

'There would never have been a right way to go about it,' she snapped, and banged her mug down. Time to throw her bags in her car and get out of here. It was a long drive to Auckland, and she intended on dropping in on her parents first.

'So you'd rather have continued being married to a man who was no longer in love with you just so you could feel righteous. What about your feelings for Luca? Are you going to walk away from them? Not fight for him, show him how much you love him?'

Ellie's mouth fell open. What? 'Have you gone crazy?'

'Probably.' Renee's stance softened and she pushed the mug of untouched coffee back towards Ellie. 'But you know me, never one to keep my mouth zipped.'

'I thought I liked that about you.'

'Changed your mind?' Renee smiled. 'When was the last time you saw Caitlin? Talked to her?'

Months ago when she'd been in a shop trying on leather jackets Caitlin had strolled in with a friend to look through the racks of clothes on sale. Ellie had tugged out of the jacket she'd been admiring in the full-length mirror, left it on the counter and stormed outside, ignoring Caitlin's pleas to stop and talk. 'The last time I said a word to her was January. When I demanded she get out of my bed, out of my house and away from my husband.' That had been the day she'd learned that the house no longer appealed to her and her husband wasn't really hers in anything but name. She'd ditched the name by the end of the day.

'Go see her.'

Ellie gasped. 'Next you'll be telling me to forgive her.'

Renee shrugged. 'If that's what it takes.'

'To do what?' This conversation was getting out of hand, but she couldn't help herself wanting to know where her friend was headed with it.

'What happened with Luca?' Renee asked.

'He sent me packing, said we had no future together.'

'And you came away. Didn't fight for him. Oh, Ellie, you need to sort your stuff out. Starting with Caitlin and Freddy.'

Ellie couldn't get Renee's words out of her head as she drove north. It hadn't helped that Mum and Dad had asked her to give her sister a call sometime. Everyone made her feel as if she were the guilty party. That she'd gone off and had an affair behind her husband's back with someone close to him instead of how it had really gone down.

You need to sort your stuff out. Renee might be back there in Wellington but her damned criticisms were in the car, going to Auckland with her.

Luca had told her to drop the ball of pain directing her life. *It's not pain.* She slapped the steering wheel with her palm. *It's anger.*

Actually it was red-hot, belly-tightening rage. The people she loved most in the world hurt her. Freddy. Caitlin. And now Luca. They did it so effortlessly. They picked her up, then tossed her aside as they chose.

Only one reason for that. She let them.

She needed windscreen wipers for her eyes. The road ahead was a blur. Lifting her foot from the accelerator, she aimed for the side of the road and parked on a narrow grass verge.

Every time she had pangs of longing to see her sister, to talk with her, she turned them into a ball of hate and hurt, put the blame squarely on Caitlin. Shoved the past aside: the nights when they'd sat in bed together talking about the guys they'd dated, the drones they'd dumped, the bullies at school or the teachers they'd hated. The clothes they'd shared—mostly Caitlin's because she had such great style, with the added bonus of being in on bargains at the right places because of her modelling career.

The tears became a torrent. 'Do you miss me, Caitlin? Like I miss you? What did I do wrong that you had to fall in love with my husband?'

Tap, tap. Ellie looked up to find a traffic cop standing beside her door. Flicking the ignition one notch, she pressed the button to open her window. 'Yes, Officer?'

'Is there a problem, ma'am?'

Quite a few actually. 'No. Am I parked illegally?'

'No, but it's not the safest place to pull over if you didn't have to.' The woman was staring at her, no doubt taking in her tear-stained scarlet cheeks. Her mascara was probably everywhere but on her lashes by now.

Ellie stared around, saw she had stopped only metres from a sharp corner. 'I was in a hurry to stop, I wasn't thinking clearly.' Would the cop stop her from driving on, or hurry her away from here?

'Can I see your licence?' When Ellie widened her eyes the cop explained, 'Routine. I have to ask every time I stop a driver.'

Ellie handed the licence over. While she waited for the cop to go check her details on the car's computer she blew her nose, finger combed her messy hair and tried to wipe away the black smudges of mascara staining her upper cheeks.

'Thank you, Doctor.' The licence appeared through the window.

'That was quick,' Ellie commented.

'I've just had a call. There's been an accident two kilometres further up this road. Truck versus car. An ambulance has been called but it will take a long while to arrive. Could you help in the meantime? I'll take you with me.' Her thumb jerked in the direction of the blue-and-yellow-striped car with the lights still flashing.

'Of course.' Ellie was already closing the window and grabbing her handbag to hide in the boot. Vehicular accidents were the thing at the moment—for her at least.

The speedy trip had Ellie's heart racing and her mouth smiling. 'I should've been a traffic cop.'

Rose—she'd given her name as they set out on this crazy ride—laughed. 'I'm not supposed to admit this, but I love the high-speed moments.' Then her smile switched off. 'Until I get to the accident and have to see all that gore. I couldn't do your job for all the money in the world.'

'So we're both doing what we enjoy, though I still hate the sight of mangled bodies. Usually I get them when they've been straightened out on a stretcher, not shoved awkwardly into a car well or around a steering wheel.'

Rose weaved around the stationary traffic already forming a long queue. 'Look at that. This isn't going to be pretty.'

Ellie had already taken in the car squashed under the front of a stock truck. 'How can anyone survive that?' she asked as she pushed out of the car. 'The car roof is flattened down on top of the occupants.'

Making her way directly to the accident site, she looked around to see if anyone had been pulled from the wreckage, saw only a brawny man standing with another traffic cop answering questions and rubbing his arms continuously.

'Hey, you can't go there,' someone called out. 'I'm a doctor.'

'She's with me,' Rose added from directly behind her.

'You don't have to come any closer,' Ellie told her. 'You go do the traffic thing and I'll see what I can do for the driver of this car.'

Two men stood up from the driver's side, allowing her access. 'We've found two men in the front. No one in the back,' one of them told her.

The driver's head was tipped back at an odd angle and his eyes were wide-open. Not good. Ellie felt sure he was deceased but she went through the motions in case. The carotid vein had no pulse. Nor was there any at his wrist. Leaning close, she listened for any sound of breathing. Nothing. Gently closing his eyelids, she looked across to the other seat at a young man also not moving.

Then his lip quivered. Just the smallest of movements, but movement nonetheless. Thankful she'd seen it, Ellie reached over to find his carotid and sighed with relief when she felt the thready beat of his pulse. How long that would last considering how much blood there was seeping from under his shoulder was a moot point. 'This man's alive,' she called as she gently probed his chest to ascertain if his ribs were broken. A punctured lung would not help his chances of survival. Nothing to indicate a rib forced into the lung cavity, but she'd go warily as only an X-ray would confirm that. 'Can we get his door open?'

'We've tried but it's stuck,' she was told.

'Then, we need to move this man out so I can get to his passenger.' Standing up, she eyeballed the two men who'd been here when she'd arrived. 'He's gone, I'm afraid, so this won't be pleasant for either of you, but the other man needs help. Fast.'

'There's a tarpaulin on the truck we can wrap him in,' a policeman said. 'Let's get this guy out of here so you can work some magic.'

Magic. She hoped her imaginary urn was full of that, because it really looked as if the passenger was going to need it all and then some. She said, 'Rose mentioned an ambulance was on its way but this man needs to get to hospital fast.'

'I told them back at base to get the rescue helicopter out here, but it still takes time for the crew to scramble and get airborne.'

'Yes, but at least they'll get him to where he needs to be faster than if he goes by road.'

'Exactly.'

Ellie steadied herself. This was so different from the accident in Laos where everyone had relied on the help of passers-by. There this man wouldn't have had a chance; here he might. 'I don't want to shift him out of that space without a neck brace and a backboard. We really need the car opened up.'

'That's our cue.' A large man dressed in a fireman's uniform stood beside the car, holding a set of Jaws of Life in one hand. 'We've got a first-aid bag with your brace. And a board.'

'Our man's chances have just gone up a notch.' Ellie wished the words back the moment they left her mouth. Talk about tempting fate. She crawled inside the mangled wreck and tried not to listen to the screeching metal as it was slowly and carefully removed by the firemen, and instead concentrated on finding the source of all that blood.

One of the firemen leaned in from the new gap in the car's exterior. 'Tell me what you require from the kit and I'll hand it through.'

Once again she was doing the emergency medicine she'd trained for in very different circumstances from what she was used to. Her admiration for ambulance crews and firemen rose higher than ever.

After an interminable time when Ellie despaired of that flying machine ever arriving it was suddenly all over. She stood with hands on her waist watching the helicopter lift off the road with her patient. 'That's that, then.'

Beside her, Rose shook her head. 'Now the fun really starts. We've got to get this lot moving again.' She nodded towards the traffic, many with their motors already running. 'I wonder how far out the coroner's vehicle is. The sooner we get that other man taken away, the sooner we can investigate the scene and open the road completely.'

Sadness rolled through Ellie. A man had died

here today because, according to the truck driver, he'd come round the corner halfway across the median line. Because of that there were going to be people whose lives would never be the same again. People that the police had yet to go and break the sad news to. 'It's so heartbreaking.' The speed at which lives could be taken, or others altered, was shocking. Everyone should hug their loved ones every day.

'I'll get someone to take you back to your car,' Rose said.

Ellie looked around, saw the impatient drivers desperate to get going, the firemen pulling what remained of the car free of the truck, the police working hard to sort everything out, and felt humble. 'You know what? I'll walk. It was only a couple of kilometres.'

'What if that had been Luca?' Ellie asked herself as she strode along the grass verge. They'd argued and were in disagreement over where their relationship should go from here on in, but he was fit and healthy back in Laos. She could talk to him just by picking up her phone. She could even hop on a flight and be able to see him, touch him, in less than twenty-four hours. She could tell him she loved him. But the family and friends of that young man had lost those opportunities forever.

Why she was thinking like this now, today, she had no idea. It wasn't as though death was new to her. She'd seen it in the department far too often. Probably the fact that she was already feeling despondent over Luca had made this worse. He'd been the first face to pop into her mind when she'd seen that crash site.

Her phone vibrated in her back pocket. It was her mother texting.

Are you safe? Caitlin's worried, says there's been a fatal accident near Levin.

Ellie pressed the phone icon. 'Hey, Mum, I'm fine. Got caught up in the traffic jam but should be on my way any moment.' Not a lie, just stretching the truth. She didn't want to say she'd been attending to the victims, didn't want to hear her mother's questions.

Her car was around the next corner.

'Mum, I've got to get going. I'll call you when

I get to Auckland if it's not too late.' Which it probably would be now. She might have to look at other options. 'Love you.'

Flicking her automatic key lock, she slipped into her car. The last thing she felt like was driving for the next eight hours. A shower would be good. She could stop halfway at Taupo, hole up in a motel for the night.

She tapped her phone. Caitlin had told Mum. Caitlin. Should she let it all go? Forgive Caitlin? No way. How could she do that? The betrayal had been huge.

But so was the void in her heart. Damn it, but she missed her sister. Caitlin had told Mum she was worried about her today.

Another worrying thought struck Ellie. Was her anger and grief over her failed marriage going to hold her back from achieving more with her career, with finding love again?

You love Luca.

Yeah, she did, but could she trust herself with that love? There was that rebound theory spinning around her skull. What if she took a chance and ended up flat on her backside again in a few months' time?

That particular risk was always there. Look at her and Freddy. She'd believed that was forever. Big mistake. Or bad judgement? Or— Drawing air into her lungs, Ellie slowly let the disturbing idea enter her mind. Had she not loved Freddy as much as she'd believed? Look how soon she'd fallen for Luca. Less than a year since her world had imploded and she was in love with him. She'd been quick to believe Freddy hadn't loved her as fervently as he'd claimed in the beginning. But what if she hadn't loved Freddy as much as she was capable of? As much as she now loved Luca?

Have I always been a little bit in love with him? So what if I have? Neither of us recognised it, so nothing was lost.

Except she'd made the mistake of marrying Freddy.

Her husband—the man her sister had fallen in love with and wanted to wed as soon as it was legally possible, and whom until now Ellie had been determined to hate for that.

Ellie turned the key so that she could lower the window and let in fresh air. She wasn't ready to start driving.

Luca had hurt her with his quick denial of their relationship. He wasn't prepared to give a little on his stance, wasn't ready to take a chance with her.

Yeah, well, she hadn't been rushing in to hug her sister and say she understood. Because she didn't understand how someone that close could fall for her husband. But— Always a damned but. Caitlin did love Freddy. She got that. Had heard her parents talk about it, had learned that Caitlin and Freddy had moved in together months ago and were as happy as sparrows in a puddle.

A shiver rocked Ellie. The skin on her forearms lifted in bumps. Was she stuck in a holding pattern? Unable to forgive and move forward, unwilling to let it all go and take control of her life again? As if she was afraid of something. Hard to believe that.

But she wasn't ready for Luca, for sure. She needed to sort herself out and get back on track before she could expect him to become a part of her life. He'd been right to tell her to go home, away from him. She was not ready. She had a lot to do first—starting now.

Ellie pulled on the handbrake and let the engine idle. Staring up at the small house on the side of the hill in central Wellington, she felt her heart almost throttling her. Her hands gripped the steering wheel so tight her knuckles were white.

Could she do this?

She had to.

It was time, way past time, really.

This was the first step of her recovery.

Still she sat staring beyond her car at the quiet suburban street. Nothing like she'd ever have believed Caitlin would choose to live in. Her sister had been about fancy apartments and patios, not overgrown lawns and tumbledown houses that had been built in the 1930s.

Move your butt.

Ellie sighed. Yep, she was procrastinating because that was way easier than facing up to Caitlin. But until she did she wasn't going anywhere with her life.

Shoving her door wide, Ellie clambered out quickly, not allowing herself a change of mind. The concrete steps leading up to the front door were uneven and crumbling at the edges. The grass hadn't seen a lawnmower in months. So unlike either of the two people living in this house. Trouble in paradise? She hoped not. Sincerely hoped not.

Have I done this all wrong? Should she have had it out with them way back at the beginning?

Too late. All she could do was work on moving ahead. Who knew what was out there for her? But until she settled the past she had this strong feeling that she wouldn't be finding out.

The door swung open as she raised her knuckles to knock. 'Ellie? Really?'

Ellie's heart rolled as she stared at her sister. Caitlin looked the same, yet different. More grown up. Major life crises did that to a person. 'Can I come in?' She knew there was reluctance in her voice, felt that the moment she stepped over the threshold she'd have conceded something—but that was why she was here. To start forgiving, start getting her family back, start accepting that she and Freddy had made a mistake, that they hadn't been right for each other.

Caitlin stepped back, pulling the door wide. Tears streamed down her face while hope and caution warred in her eyes. 'You were on your way to Auckland,' she finally said in a strangled voice so unlike her usually vibrant, cheeky tone.

'I'm making a detour.' Ellie ran her tongue over her suddenly dry lips, tried to still her rolling stomach that felt as if it was about to toss her breakfast. What was she doing here? This was way too hard. She hadn't forgiven anyone. *But you want to. You want your sister back.*

Caitlin turned away abruptly, almost ran down the hall towards the kitchen. 'I'll put the coffee on.'

Ellie's feet were rooted to the floor. Should she stay? Should she go? An image of the young man she'd declared deceased snapped on in her mind. Were there people out there he hadn't apologised to for something? Had he told his girlfriend or wife or kids this morning that he loved them?

She moved forward, one shaky step at a time, to the door of the kitchen. 'I've missed you.'

That wasn't what she'd meant to say at all. She'd been going to demand an explanation for why she hadn't been told about the affair. But now that she'd uttered the words her whole body started to let go the tightness that had been there since January.

The bag in Caitlin's fingers hit the floor, spraying coffee beans in every direction. Then Caitlin was leaping at her, wrapping her arms around her, crying, 'Ellie, I'm so sorry. I didn't mean to hurt you. I love you. I've missed you every day since.' Her tears soaked into Ellie's blouse as she clung to her.

Ellie couldn't stop her own tears from streaming down her face. But nor could she find any words: her throat was blocked and her brain on strike. She so wanted to forgive Caitlin, but to verbalise that didn't come easily. Didn't come at all. Finally she lifted her head and dropped her arms to her sides. 'I'll see you on Christmas Day.'

Then she left. And started her journey all over

again, this time with her heart feeling a little lighter.

Slipping a CD into the car stereo, she even hummed as she drove out of the city and along the highway past the ocean—for the second time that day. Definitely stopping the night in Taupo now. Listening to The Exponents brought other memories crowding in—all of Luca. Luca dancing. Luca laughing. Being patient with the kids at the clinic. Kissing her, making love to her. Luca. She sighed with longing clogging her senses.

What would he say if he knew she'd been to see her sister? Now she'd been to see Caitlin, would he think better of her for it? Would he work at letting go some of his hang-ups now that she'd started on hers?

Nah, of course he wouldn't. He was determined never to change, never to take a risk.

'Well, Luca, that's all fine and dandy, but I've started to turn my life around, and you can do the same, even if it doesn't bring you back to me.' She sang the words almost in tune to the song blaring from the stereo. A sad song, she realised, just as a fresh bout of tears began splashing down her face.

She'd reached Levin again, and looked around for a place to park. Strong coffee was needed. And food to stop the shakes and settle these stupid crying bursts. What was wrong with her anyway? She'd started patching things up with Caitlin, which had to be good. She might want Luca but that wasn't going to happen any time soon, if at all, and no amount of bawling her eyes out would alter that. Blowing her nose hard, she scrunched up the tissue and stepped out of the car to head for the nearest café. 'Auckland, here I come. Life, here I come.'

CHAPTER TWELVE

LUCA TOOK OVER from Aaron, suturing the wound on the right leg of their latest bomb victim while the other man drew deep breaths of air. 'It never gets any easier, does it?'

'No,' growled Aaron. 'What I wouldn't like to do to those bastards that left the bombs lying around in the first place.'

'Come on, Aaron. We've had this discussion a dozen times. You know there's nothing to do about it except what you already do.' Louise's eyes were on their patient but her words were with her husband. 'You're getting yourself all wound up again.'

Luca concentrated on his work. He'd spent many hours lying awake at night thinking about what the Laotian people had to live with but understood there was nothing he could do to remove all those bombs. The suture needle clattered into the kidney dish and he straightened his back, feeling the aches from the continuous bending over. Doctoring was what he did, had spent years learning how to do, but he hoped he'd never see another damaged limb, never perform another amputation.

'Let's wrap this up,' Aaron said.

'Could go for a plate of sticky rice and peanut sauce right about now,' Luca replied as his stomach rumbled. Dinner had been hours ago, a meal they'd barely had a mouthful of before rushing into Theatre with this teenaged boy.

Louise shook her head at him. 'Nothing puts you off your food, does it?'

'Not much.' Except Ellie. Since she'd left after giving him a speech on how she thought he should be living his life, he hadn't been as interested in food as usual. Nor in beer, sightseeing or playing cricket with the kids. It felt as if she'd taken the sun with her. Everything—or maybe only he—was gloomy. Downright depressing some days. He'd gone and fallen in love with her. Like really, deeply in love. The sort of love he'd always known he was capable of and determined not to have.

Let go some of that control, she'd railed at him. If only Ellie knew how much self-discipline he'd lost over the weeks since he'd first seen her with Louise on the day she arrived. Try as hard as he could, he wasn't getting it back. He wasn't able to push aside his love for her, no matter how it burned him to try. He did not want to love Ellie. It broke the rod he'd used for living his whole life. Snapped it clean in two. He still didn't want to love and yet now he did.

So all he had to do was ignore it, and hope that eventually he'd be able to manage getting through an hour at a time without thinking about Ellie, without wondering where she was and what she was doing. Wondering if she missed him half as much as he did her. Hoping for her sake she didn't, and pleading with the stars for his sake she did.

What a mess he'd become.

'Let's go into town for a beer and that rice you're hankering after,' Aaron said as they pulled off their scrubs. 'Louise will stay with the boy, and Jason's here if there's any change in his condition.'

Jason. The next doctor in a long line of short-term doctors. The guy was cool, eager to help and join in all the fun with the kids, was a better bowler of the cricket ball than Ellie had been— but he wasn't El. 'Good idea.' Anything to take his mind off her for a few minutes.

But so much for that theory. Aaron plonked two bottles on the counter in a bar they used occasionally on Sethathirath Road. 'Heard from Ellie lately?'

'No. You or Louise?'

'Got an email yesterday. She was heading to Auckland today. Guess she'll be there by now. How far is it from Wellington?'

'It'll take all day. Though with Ellie at the wheel you can cut an hour off the time.' Unless she'd quietened down recently. He wouldn't know. Didn't know a lot of things about the woman he loved, when he thought about it. Which was all the damned time.

'Bit of a speedster, is she?'

'She had this fire-engine-red Mustang that she

got a kick out of taking for a spin. That thing went like a scalded cat, only with a lot more revs. It was her pride and joy, and her only real indulgence. Cost her a bundle in speeding tickets, though.' *Wonder what happened to it.*

Aaron was lifting one eyebrow in his direction.

'What?' he demanded.

'You're smiling for the first time since Ellie left.'

'Of course it's not the first time.' He raised his beer to his lips. He always smiled and laughed, didn't he? Right now he felt relaxed and happy because of those memories. Yeah, but when was the last time he'd felt remotely like this?

Aaron shook his head at him. 'I must've been looking the other way.' Then he changed the subject. 'You made up your mind where you're going after Laos?'

While it was a different topic, it still brought Luca back to Ellie. Hopping a ride down to New Zealand was at the top of his list. Seeing Ellie would be the best thing to happen to him since she'd left. Then what? He'd have to leave again.

They couldn't return to a platonic friendship after that mind-blowing night in Luang Prabang. Even he knew that. So staying on in Auckland, which was the only city he wanted to work in at home, was not an option. It might be a large city but Ellie would be there and he'd never be able to forget that, always be looking for her.

He told Aaron, 'I'm liking the look of Cambodia.' Sort of. Though returning to his career as an emergency specialist seemed to be teasing him more and more every day. 'Maybe Australia.' Closer to home and more in line with his career ideas.

'If you're thinking of Cambodia why not stay here for the next twelve months? Not a lot of difference, when it comes to working with the locals, if you think about it.' Aaron had tried to convince him of this on several occasions, and was now flagrantly ignoring the Australian component of his reply.

Luca's phone vibrated in his pocket. Pulling it out, he saw he had two texts. 'Noi says our boy's doing fine.'

Aaron grunted. 'I got that, too.'

Luca's mouth dried. Ellie had texted him hours ago. He hadn't checked his phone after they'd finished in Theatre. Hadn't thought there'd be any messages.

Visited Caitlin today. Late leaving Wellington for Auckland, stopping over in Taupo. How's everyone at the clinic? Ellie. XXX

'Wow. Ellie visited her sister.' That took guts.

'What's so odd about that?' Aaron asked.

Damn, he hadn't meant to speak out loud. 'They've been estranged all year. Like, seriously.' But Ellie had gone to see her. Had taken the gauntlet he'd thrown down to get on with sorting out her life. Good on her.

What about the challenge she set you?

What about it?

Going to run with it? Or away from it?

'That's sad, but Ellie's obviously had a change of heart.' Aaron was watching him closely. Looking for what?

'They used to be very close.' It wouldn't be easy talking to anyone who'd had an affair with her husband, but Caitlin? She hadn't said how it had gone. They might've had an even bigger bust-up, but he didn't think she'd be telling him if that was the case. 'I don't know if the girls will ever get back what they had.'

'Christmas is only one week away. That's always a good time for families to be together.'

Ellie would hate spending the day on her own. Christmas had always been a big deal for her. 'What do we do here for Christmas? Get a tree and lots of presents for the kids?' They would this year, if he had anything to do with it.

'All of that and loads of food, though it's hard to find anything like what we're used to back home. You going to be here?'

'Why wouldn't I be?' The guy knew he had less than two months to run on his contract.

Aaron stared at something across the other side of the bar. 'Thought you might want to go spend it with Ellie.'

Luca spluttered the mouthful of beer he'd just taken. 'You what?'

An eloquent shrug came his way. 'Most men I know would do almost anything to be with the woman they love for Christmas.'

Luca wanted to deny it, wanted to shout at the top of his lungs that Aaron didn't have a clue what he was talking about. But he couldn't. *Because it was true.* Which didn't lessen the urge to hurl his bottle across the room and shout at somebody. Gritting his teeth, he held on to his sanity—just. Counted to ten, again and again. When he finally believed he could speak without spitting he said, 'That obvious, huh?'

'Neon.'

'Great.' So everyone knew what had taken him four weeks to work out. Or was that ten years? Had he always loved Ellie? That little gem didn't feel wrong. Or a shock. Maybe he had. Talk about a slow learner.

'What are you going to do about it?'

Any time you want to shut up, Aaron, I'm not going to stop you. 'Nothing.'

'Fair enough.'

Huh? What sort of answer was that? 'How long did you know Louise before you realised you loved her?'

'Minutes. It was as though she hit me over the head or something. Instant, man.' A smile lit up

Aaron's eyes. 'Never regretted it for a second. Not even when she burns my bacon.'

'True love,' Luca drawled. 'No challenges, then. No problems to get over before you got together permanently?'

'Ha. A ton of them. But we weren't going to be deterred by anything. Life's too short, as that accident you were in shows. What would you have felt if Ellie hadn't made it out of that van? Think you might've spent the rest of your life regretting not telling her how you feel?'

'I think you make a better doctor than a psychologist.'

Aaron picked up their empty bottles. 'Another?'

'Sure. Why not?' Luca picked up his phone and tapped the screen, reread El's text. Short and to the point. Why had she contacted him when they'd more or less agreed to go their separate ways when she'd left Vientiane? She'd have struggled to visit Caitlin, and it wasn't something she'd have done just to prove a point so she must just be keeping in touch, treating him like the close friend he'd insisted he was.

He'd been adamant they weren't getting together and she'd got the message, loud and clear. She'd even said how she wondered if this had been a rebound thing. Sex with a man she knew well and could trust to look out for her. Yet at the same time she knew he had his limitations and would never ask her to set up house with him.

Control, she called that. Told him to let it go. Hell, if he did who knew when he'd stop unravelling? Everything he'd struggled to gain would go down the drain. Right now he was out of plans for the next year or two; let go of that control Ellie despised so much and he would be lost forever.

Ellie didn't sound lost after seeing Caitlin.

He wasn't really thinking when he began tapping in a message.

How did it go with Caitlin? Did you talk?

The moment he sent the text he wanted it back. Getting involved wasn't his greatest idea. Before he knew it he'd be wanting to be there to help Ellie through the minefield that getting back onside with Caitlin entailed. How would El handle seeing her sister with her ex? Then he saw the time. She wasn't going to read it for hours yet. It was early morning back in NZ. He had a few hours to regret his move.

We hugged. I made a date for Christmas and left.

Got that wrong. Was she lying awake worrying about her sister?

Christmas is good. Family time. Why are you awake?

Might as well ask since he'd started this.
She came straight back: Missing you.
Right then Aaron slid a beer in front of him. Perfect timing. 'Thanks.' He closed the phone and slid it into his pocket. He had no reply to that text. Not one that he was prepared to make. That would mean laying his heart on the line.

Christmas was a week away, right? Luca stretched his legs to increase his pace as he strode along the path winding beside the Mekong. Seven days, to be exact. Then it would be over and life could go back to normal.
Except Christmas wasn't going to be nor-

mal for Ellie, which meant the days afterwards wouldn't be, either. Spending time with her family would be hard, and if Baldwin was there, which he had to presume he would be, then, hell, Ellie was in for a terrible day.

She needed support. But who from? He was here, and fighting the urge to give in to go home for a few days. He coughed. Time to start being really honest with himself. It was the need to see Ellie that he was fighting. Acknowledging he loved her hadn't taken the edge off that need. It had made him supercautious when answering any more of her many texts. El hadn't taken a back step when he'd told her to go home and get on with her life without him. Oh, no.

Pulling his phone from his pocket, he went through the past three texts. His pace slowed as he reread the challenge she kept waving in his face.

How are the kids? Say hi to them from me. Missing them and you.

Of course every time he mentioned Ellie to the kids he'd be bombarded with questions about where was she, when was she coming back and could they all text her, too—on his phone? Kids. He'd seen the hunger in her eyes at Luang Prabang Airport as she'd held that baby; the hunger that had wormed into him and made him think about having children with Ellie. Him? Having kids? El had said he was good with children, but how far could he take that?

Won't know if I don't try. Suddenly that idea didn't seem so impossible. With Ellie by his side he could conquer seemingly insurmountable problems. She was his rock, believed in him—knew him too well, which was grounds for a solid relationship. Wasn't it?

The next text.

How's your nephew? Missing you.

She knew damned well he didn't have any contact with his sister's kid. Did she think he'd suddenly start emailing the lad because she thought he should? Of course she did. She was challenging him to sort his life out. As she'd started to do with hers.

Then the text that had thrown him when he'd first read it.

Saw the house I'm moving into for six months. It's stunning and has me thinking about buying my own here in Auckland. Missing you.

Two decisions in one sentence. Buying a house spoke of putting down roots, and obviously she was happy to be back in Auckland. Far enough away from her family to avoid awkward get-to-gethers but close enough to see them occasionally if she felt so inclined.

Luca read that one again. Missing you. She used that at the end of every message. It hit him hard in the heart every single time. Stuffing his phone back in his pocket, he stared at the brown river pouring past in its timeless way. 'Hell, El, I'm missing you fit to bust. You'll never guess how much.'

Unless he told her. Could he do that? Find the courage to commit to her?

I want to. More than anything I want to be with Ellie Thompson for all the years to come.

Which meant some sharp gear changes in the

head. Did he have the guts to do that? Ellie had shown courage by visiting Caitlin. Somehow he had to find the same within himself.

His gaze cruised the rushing water again. Water that came from the north, through countries, towns, communities, the flow barely changing from one year to the next. The river moved on, from yesterday to tomorrow, returning to calm after floods and storms and wars, making allowances for small changes in direction. Like life.

Except his was lacking something, someone. Ellie. It spooked him to think he might've always loved her but had been too tied up in his determination to avoid commitment that he'd pushed his feelings so deep it was a wonder they'd come to light. He could try just jumping in—sort of a leap of confidence in himself and Ellie. And if it backfired? That was where the courage would come in. He'd have to start over, but was that such a bad thing when the alternative might be to never experience a wonderful relationship with the woman already sitting in his heart? He'd told Ellie to let go of what Caitlin and Freddy had done, to make some decisions for herself about herself.

Why couldn't he do the same with Gaylene? She was a shield. He stopped walking to stare up at the sky. Hell. Had he been hiding behind her? Using what she'd done to him as an excuse to stay away from getting hurt again? Because she had hurt him—badly. He mightn't have been head over heels in love with her but he'd been willing to try. He'd wanted some say in their child's life. Had been devastated when she'd terminated it with no regard to his feelings. Of course he'd been hurt and angry. But that was no reason to push Ellie away. None at all.

Another left-field thought dropped into his head. Why not follow El's example and get in touch with his sister? A friendly email with no demands, just 'hi, how are you, this is what I'm doing' stuff. If he didn't try he'd never get back the family he missed.

Ellie rolled out of bed and dropped her head in her hands. Christmas morning usually made her smile with excitement. But not this one. Her stomach was roiling, making her nauseous.

Today she had to face up to Caitlin and Freddy over Christmas lunch with Mum and Dad. Play happy families. Ugh. Why had she said she'd do this?

Because if she wanted to have a life with Luca she needed to move on. Luca. All very well for him to say she should sort herself out. What had he done about doing the same with his own life? Huh?

Fumbling on the bedside table, she found her phone and checked for messages. Nothing. Not a word from Luca for days. Guess that would teach her to keep telling him she missed him. But she'd only been truthful, even when knowing he wouldn't be comfortable with it. So much for thinking he might give in and accept she wasn't going to change her mind about loving him.

'Morning.' Renee strolled into the room looking rumpled and relaxed in her cotton PJs. 'Merry Christmas.'

Ellie jumped up and hugged her friend. 'Merry

Christmas to you. Thanks for lending me the bed.' She'd flown in late last night and come straight here, having turned down her mother's plea to stay with them. There was only so much time she'd be able to face spending with her sister and ex. She might be making headway but she wasn't ready for full-on happy families yet.

'It's still got your name on it.' Renee laughed. 'I've got the coffee brewing or there's bubbles waiting to be opened.'

'Think I'll start the day with coffee. Need to keep my head straight until after Christmas lunch is over.'

'You know you can come back here to join my lot if it all gets too much for you today.' Renee hugged her back.

'You're a great friend.' Her other great friend seemed to have forgotten all about her, not even sending a Christmas message in reply to the one she'd sent after falling into bed last night. Ellie tugged her bag close and pulled out the sundress she'd planned on wearing today. 'I'll grab a shower first.'

Renee was already half out the door. 'Don't take too long. I want to give you my present.'

But when Ellie made it to the kitchen Renee was in no hurry to hand her anything except a steaming mug of coffee after quickly putting her phone aside.

Instead, Renee made a great fuss of opening the exquisitely wrapped box that contained the opal earrings and bracelet Ellie had bought for her.

'They're gorgeous.' Renee grinned, slipping the bracelet over her hand. 'Beautiful.' She slowly removed one earring from the silk cushion it rested on and slipped it through her earlobe. As she plucked the second one up the doorbell buzzed. 'Someone's early for breakfast. Get that for me, will you? I'm heading for the bathroom.' Renee disappeared so fast Ellie didn't have a chance to say a word.

The buzzer sounded again.

'I'm coming,' she muttered and swung the door wide. 'Merry— Luca.' She looked behind him but no one else was there. None of Renee's family. Only Luca. Her heart rate stuttered, then sped up. Luca was *here*? In Wellington?

'Merry Luca. That's novel.' He grinned at her.

'Are you? Merry, I mean?' *Are you Luca? Or just a figment of my imagination?*

'Merry ho-ho, yes. Merry boozy, no.' Uncertainty replaced that grin. 'Are you going to invite me in, El?'

She stepped back so quickly she banged up against the wall. 'Renee thought one of her—' No, she hadn't. She'd been dilly-dallying over coffee and her present, then suddenly, when the buzzer went, she'd headed for the shower. 'Renee knew you were coming, didn't she?'

Luca nodded. 'Yes. I rang her to find out where you were staying. I wanted to surprise you, El.'

'You've certainly done that.' She led him into the kitchen, all the time trying to get her heart rate and breathing under control, but it seemed impossible. Luca was here, not in Laos. With her and not the children. 'Why?'

'Why am I here?' His eyebrows rose and he reached for her hands as she nodded once. 'I'm going with you to your family Christmas lunch.'

Her head shot up. 'You're what?'

'I'm going to be there for you, with you, supporting you. I know it's not going to be easy being with Caitlin and Baldwin.'

She should've been relaxing, getting excited. She wasn't. 'You're being a good friend.'

Luca stepped closer, finally taking her hands in his. 'No, El, I'm your partner.'

'What do you mean?' Was she being thick? The sense of missing something important nagged her. 'My partner? As in lover, kids, house partner?' *Or 'sex when he was in town' partner?*

His smile was gentle and—dare she admit it?—full of love. He said, 'I'm done with being just your best friend. I want the whole shebang. With you.' His hands were warm, strong yet soft. Enticing her closer.

Even as she held back, a glimmer of hope eased through her. Had Luca come because he loved her? It sounded like it. 'You stopped answering my texts and emails.'

'I'm not good with words, especially not in messages. But I missed you so much it started

driving me nuts. I had to come see you. Nothing could've kept me away any longer.'

'Have you decided what you're doing after
Laos?' What did it matter? Why was she being
so cautious?

'Moving to Auckland to be near you, or with
you if you'll have me.'

She gasped. 'Luca? What are you really saying?' Pulling her hands free, she folded her arms
across her chest. She did not want the distraction
of him holding her while she absorbed whatever
he was about to tell her.

'El—' he locked his eyes on hers '—I'm saying I love you. I've missed you since you told
me to get a life. You are my life. I want to share
everything with you. Starting with your Christmas Day.'

Now her heart was really pumping. 'Everything?' He couldn't mean that. He'd gone to
great lengths to make her understand he didn't
want the same things she did.

His hands were on her wrists, unfolding her
arms. Then he was holding her hands again,
his thumbs caressing her. 'You, the babies, the

house and cats and dogs or pet rabbits. The whole works.'

If Luca could say all that, then it was time she opened her heart and laid everything out there for him, too. 'I want all those things, too, with you. I love you so much it hurts when you're not with me. These past two weeks have been horrible.'

His arms went around her and he gently drew her close. 'Tell me about it.'

'I have missed you.'

He chuckled. 'Yeah, I got those messages loud and clear.'

'You didn't reply to them.'

'I was too afraid to. Once I told you I was missing you I'd be committed to you, and I had to be sure. I've done a lot of soul searching, but in the end I can't deny how much I love you and want you. Loving you is easier than not. I promise not to let you down.'

'Luca, I never thought you would. All that was in your head, not mine.' She gave him a little shake.

'Good answer.' He gave a lopsided smile. 'Seriously, thank you for believing in me and giving me the boot up the backside I needed to see what has been in front of me for a very long time. I've done something else, too. I emailed Ange and she replied saying to drop by while I'm here. As in visit her in Auckland, which is where you're going after today, right?'

Ellie nodded. 'Yes.'

'Then, so am I. I've finally worked out I've loved you for years. Then I had to tell you face to face. So here I am.'

Ellie reached her arms around his neck and raised up to place her mouth on his. 'Shut up for a moment.' Then she kissed him.

His arms wrapped around her, his chest hard against her breasts, his mouth open to hers. Ellie slid her tongue between his lips, tasted her man and melted further against him. Luca was here. He'd always been in her heart, but he was here in her arms, kissing her as ardently as she did him. All her Christmases had come today. All of them.

'Merry Christmas, Ellie.' Renee's voice broke through her euphoria.

Peeling her mouth off Luca's, she turned in his arms to stare at her friend. 'Best present ever.'

'That's what I thought.' Renee had the cheek to wink. 'I'm popping the champagne. What I just saw requires celebrating.'

'I agree.' Ellie grinned, finally letting all the fear and hurt and need fly. Luca loved her. What more could a girl want?

As the three of them raised their glasses Renee said, 'To Ellie and Luca.' She drained her flute and put it down. 'I'd better go and get those croissants and bagels I ordered for breakfast. My family will start arriving shortly. See you.' She waved a hand over her shoulder as she headed for her front door. There she turned around and, looking very pleased with herself, she gave Ellie a big wink. 'One hour to yourselves. Merry Christmas, my friends.'

* * * * *

MILLS & BOON®
Large Print Medical

June

Playboy Doc's Mistletoe Kiss	Tina Beckett
Her Doctor's Christmas Proposal	Louisa George
From Christmas to Forever?	Marion Lennox
A Mummy to Make Christmas	Susanne Hampton
Miracle Under the Mistletoe	Jennifer Taylor
His Christmas Bride-to-Be	Abigail Gordon

July

A Daddy for Baby Zoe?	Fiona Lowe
A Love Against All Odds	Emily Forbes
Her Playboy's Proposal	Kate Hardy
One Night...with Her Boss	Annie O'Neil
A Mother for His Adopted Son	Lynne Marshall
A Kiss to Change Her Life	Karin Baine

August

His Shock Valentine's Proposal	Amy Ruttan
Craving Her Ex-Army Doc	Amy Ruttan
The Man She Could Never Forget	Meredith Webber
The Nurse Who Stole His Heart	Alison Roberts
Her Holiday Miracle	Joanna Neil
Discovering Dr Riley	Annie Claydon

MILLS & BOON®
Large Print Medical

September

The Socialite's Secret	Carol Marinelli
London's Most Eligible Doctor	Annie O'Neil
Saving Maddie's Baby	Marion Lennox
A Sheikh to Capture Her Heart	Meredith Webber
Breaking All Their Rules	Sue MacKay
One Life-Changing Night	Louisa Heaton

October

Seduced by the Heart Surgeon	Carol Marinelli
Falling for the Single Dad	Emily Forbes
The Fling That Changed Everything	Alison Roberts
A Child to Open Their Hearts	Marion Lennox
The Greek Doctor's Secret Son	Jennifer Taylor
Caught in a Storm of Passion	Lucy Ryder

November

Tempted by Hollywood's Top Doc	Louisa George
Perfect Rivals...	Amy Ruttan
English Rose in the Outback	Lucy Clark
A Family for Chloe	Lucy Clark
The Doctor's Baby Secret	Scarlet Wilson
Married for the Boss's Baby	Susan Carlisle

0516 LP 2P P2 Medical